PETTERIL'S
Ladybird
MARY LANCASTER

Petteril's Ladybird

Lord Petteril Mysteries, Book 3

Mary Lancaster

Petteril's Ladybird

Table of Contents

Chapter One

A pall of thick fog hung over London as Piers Withan, fifth Viscount Petteril, returned to his town house in May. Cold and damp as he undoubtedly was, he could not help comparing this arrival with his last, just over two months ago. Then, the house had been unoccupied, bare, and bleak, a symbol of grief and the unbearable life being forced upon him.

Now, he actually grinned as the girl beside him, April, leapt out of the curricle to get to the horses' heads moments before the footman ran out to take them. He could not cure her of the habit and wasn't sure he wanted to.

He alighted with marginally more grace, spared a pat for the near-horse's neck and strolled into his house.

"Welcome home, my lord," his impressive butler, greeted him with what appeared to be a genuine smile.

Piers had employed him largely because his eyes occasionally twinkled. He could not abide Friday-faced butlers. "Thank you, Park. I trust everyone is well?"

"Indeed, sir. I hope your journey was not too trying?"

"Not until we reached London and the fog blinded us!"

"Sir Peter Haggard awaits you in the library, my lord," Park said, taking Piers's hat and coat and passing them to the waiting footman. "He said you were expecting him. Would you prefer to bathe and change before you receive him?"

"No, I'll do that afterward. Good day, Mrs. Park," he added cheerfully to the housekeeper who beamed at him.

"I'll send up tea and toast," she said.

Piers was surprised to find tea and toast was exactly what he wanted to scare the chill from his bones, so he grinned back at her and leapt upstairs, three at a time.

He was glad to find the library fire had been lit, though it was with more mixed feelings that he greeted his visitor who, in fact, was the one who had summoned him back to London from his country estate.

"Haggs," Piers said, holding out his hand, which Haggard strode over to shake.

"Withy!" His friend's harsh-featured face showed deep concern behind his grin. "Sorry to annoy you as soon as you're over the doorstep, but I thought you'd want to know. It looks bad for Austen."

"What happened?" Piers waved him to a chair. "Who the devil do they think he killed?"

"Barret Bootle."

"Er...should I know the name?"

"No, he's several years older than us. Younger son of the Earl of Kinsley."

"Hence the danger. Why the devil do they think it was Percy Austen? Amiable fellow, Percy."

"Got a temper, though," Haggard said judiciously. "All the same, I'm sure he didn't do this. Trouble is, he quarrelled with Bootle the same day. You and I know if he was going to attack someone, he'd have done it then—or at least called Bootle out. Not gone home, brooded for several hours and then returned to shoot him in the back of the head."

Piers winced. "No. That doesn't sound like the Percy Austen I remember. What did they quarrel over?"

Haggard grimaced. "A woman. One Mrs. Eastleigh, a taking little widow whom Austen installed in a pleasant house in Kensington a few years ago. They parted ways last year and I believe Bootle took over the lease of both house and widow."

A footman brought in a heavy tray of tea things and a mountainous plate of toast. He smiled too, a welcome relief from the squalid little tale being told. His name was Francis and it was a pleasure as well as a small triumph to recognize his face.

"Go on," Piers said, when Francis had gone. He threw himself into the chair opposite his friend. "Where did the shooting happen?"

"In Mrs. Eastleigh's house," Haggs said grimly.

"Then isn't it more likely to have been Mrs. Eastleigh?"

"Her maid claims to have been with her when it happened. Besides..."

Piers felt a tightening in his stomach. This, he suspected, was the crux of the matter. "Besides what?" he asked with a sense of doom.

"The pistol he was shot with belonged to Austen. It was found next to the body and Austen admitted it was his."

Piers stared at him. "He left it there like a banner? A signature, acknowledging *I did this*?"

Haggard shrugged. "Stupid, I know. But the magistrate seems to think it suits a crime of such passion, even if he hasn't yet arrested him for it. Percy denies it, of course. And it's hardly the crime of a gentleman."

"Then why is he being pursued for it? Are the Bootles out for blood?"

"It would appear so."

Piers drank his tea and munched his way through a slice of toast and butter.

"What do you think we should do for him?" Haggard wondered. "Except try and find him a top-of-the-trees barrister."

Piers scowled. "We can't let it come to trial. He has a sister and an aunt and God knows how many dependents. Even if he got off, they'd all be ruined."

"I'm open to suggestion."

Piers put down his teacup and rose to pull the bell. "Send me Miss April," he said to the footman who appeared, and to Haggard, "She's good at stuff like this."

Haggard regarded him while he swallowed his last mouthful of toast. "Miss *April*," he repeated. "Surely you don't mean...?"

April herself breezed into the room like the sun breaking through a cloud. "Whatcher, sir?" she greeted Haggard with a grin. Even in an old-fashioned, unflattering dress, with a maid's cap crammed over her too-short golden locks, she was dazzling when she smiled.

"Good God," Haggard said.

Piers watched with some pride as recognition and then wonder filled his friend's ugly-attractive countenance.

"Oh dear," Haggard uttered.

"What d'you mean, *oh dear*?" April demanded. "I got jam on me face, or what?"

"Lord, no," Haggard said, recovering. "You look charmingly, I assure you."

April wrinkled her slightly upturned nose. "I know he told you, so there's no need to stare."

"Still as cheeky as Ape," Haggard remarked. "What on earth do the other servants say?"

"Nothing. They can't imagine it, especially 'cause I'm *Miss* April now, *his* assistant."

Piers interrupted. "We're going out in half an hour and you had better come with us. You'll have to wash and change."

She looked him up and down. "So will you."

"Indeed," he murmured as she all but skipped off. He kept his face bland and, he hoped, colour-free, as he faced Haggard once more.

Haggs said, "I congratulate you on the transformation. But you do know what people will say?"

Piers sighed. "Gossip dies from lack of oxygen. We've already been through it at Haybury Court."

"Maybe so, but you can't take her into Austen's aunt's drawing room with you!"

Piers considered. "All things are possible," he said vaguely. Then, seeing Haggard's expression, he added, "You know damned well I haven't touched her. And wouldn't."

"Won't stop other men from trying."

"Well, they're liable to get more than they bargained for," Piers said with a twisted smile.

"Hmm." Haggard reached for another slice of toast. The mountain on the plate was severely reduced. "What is she, though? She's no stable lad anymore, and she doesn't behave like any maid I've ever come across. What the devil is an assistant?"

Piers considered. "One who assists. Like a secretary. Or a governess. Only she eats in the servants' hall, so I suppose she is an upper servant. Mrs. Park knows all about her."

"Do *you*?" Haggard asked, genuine anxiety in his eyes. After all, April had been living rough on the streets of St. Giles as a boy before Piers had employed her in his stable.

Piers was glad he had never told his friend that on their first encounter, April had been burgling his house. "I know enough," he said, making for the door. "I'll be twenty minutes."

April, although she would have liked a longer gossip over a cup of tea in Mrs. Park's cosy sitting room, was excited to be off on another mystery with Lord Petteril. Sir Peter Haggard came with them in the new town carriage, recently bought to replace the one borrowed on a permanent basis and without permission by Petteril's aunt, the Dowager Lady Petteril.

In a fresh white linen cap and a new—to April—dark green dress, her leather bag at her waist containing her notebook and pencil and a few things she would rather his lordship remain unaware of, she sat opposite the men, her back to the horses to show her lowly status. About which, she cared nothing at all. Between them, Lord Petteril and Sir Peter told her about the murder of Lord Kinsley's son, the Honourable Barret Bootle, in the home of his ladybird, a widow no better than she should be, according to Sir Peter's austere description.

"Everyone got to survive," April told him, thinking of her own old friend Annie, a prostitute who'd been kind to her in St. Giles before escaping to one rich cove who'd given her a whole house of her own. Now April had got out, too, and still couldn't quite believe her luck. The half-starved lad once at the beck and call of petty thieves and villains, now rode in a carriage with gentlemen who *wanted* her opinion, rather than backhanding her when she had gall to give it for free. "So can't this friend of yours just tell the beak he was somewhere else?"

"He can't prove he was," Sir Peter said with a sigh.

The sun seemed to be trying hard to penetrate the fog as they alighted in front of another posh town house. Though not as big as Petteril's, it could still have lodged many families in St. Giles or Whitechapel.

In the absence of orders to the contrary, April trailed after the others to the front door. A footman admitted them at once, although he glared at April, raising his hand to point through the front door to the area steps and the servants' entrance.

Deftly, she dropped her cloak over his hand. "Thank you," she said with her sweetest smile and sailed after his lordship across the hall to a small library occupied by two people. A worried looking young gentleman sprang to his feet, a smile clearing the anxiety from his face as he flung out his hand to Lord Petteril. April had noticed he had this effect on most people. Apart from his family, of course, who didn't deserve him.

"Withy! What a pleasure to see you again! Or should I call you *my lord* these days?"

"Only every second sentence," Petteril replied, warmly shaking the offered hand. "I am quite full enough of my own consequence."

The gentleman's grin broadened as he looked his guest up and down. "So I see. What happened to the rumpled scholar I last saw blinking at unexpected daylight?" He lifted both Petteril's quizzing glasses between fingers and thumbs. "*Poseur.*"

"One needs to see," Petteril said with dignity.

His friend snorted. Then, as the lady behind him rose from the table, blushing slightly, he turned to her. Her features were enough like Austen's to proclaim their relationship, although her hair was a shade darker, and she must have been about five or six years younger. She wore a very becoming morning gown of pure white.

Austen said, "Do you remember my sister Louise? Lou, Withy is Lord Petteril now! And I believe you know Sir Peter Haggard."

He stepped aside, as Petteril moved to bow over the lady's hand, and finally caught sight of April. Sir Peter smiled lazily and said nothing.

"Ah, hope you don't mind," Lord Petteril said, becoming aware of the brother and sister's consternation. "I brought my assistant, April. April, this is Mr. Austen, and his sister Miss Austen."

April bobbed a curtsey.

Her hosts looked baffled, though they nodded acknowledgement.

"Why do you need an assistant?" Mr. Austen asked.

"She is useful in many matters, including proving the innocence of fellows otherwise heading for the gallows."

That at least wiped the impending outrage from Austen's face, although his sister whitened alarmingly and clutched at the table behind her.

"If that was meant to be a jest, my lord, it was in poor taste," she uttered.

And his lordship actually blushed. "I beg your pardon. It was indeed poor taste." He hurried on as though both chastened and embarrassed, which didn't quite please April, although it was interesting. "Percy, you had better tell me everything. When did this Bootle fellow die?"

Miss Austen had pulled herself together and invited everyone to sit. April took the chair by the door and took out her notebook and pencil, turning rapidly to a clean page. Her writing had improved immensely in the last few weeks and she was rather proud of it. Even though her speed was nothing like his lordship's.

"He died last Monday," Percy Austen said morosely. He was a good-looking young man with fashionably short, light brown hair. His eyes and mouth seemed more kind than decisive. "Around midnight, I'm told."

"Why is it always a Monday?" Petteril murmured, though only April understood, since it had been a Monday night that the man in his lordship's wood at Haybury had been murdered. "And where were you when it happened?"

"Here," Austen replied, waving one hand at the sofa where Petteril and Sir Peter now sat. "I fell asleep. I—er... I'd had a little too much to drink."

"Why?" Petteril asked.

Austen glanced at his sister. "Louise, perhaps you could order tea for our guests? And make sure Aunt Moll doesn't try to join us?"

Louise cast him a scornful glance, but she did rise once more, curtsey to the guests and walk out.

"Bit awkward with one's sister sitting there," Austen remarked. "Thing is, I went to call on Mrs. Eastleigh that morning, just to make sure she was well, you understand."

"Perfectly," Sir Peter said wryly. "Was she?"

"Oh yes. But Barret Bootle was there, too. Being dashed unpleasant, to be honest. Implied I had no right to be there since he now paid the lease. I said I was merely calling on an old friend from courtesy, but he assumed I was trying to have my cake and eat it, as it were, at his expense. We quarrelled loudly enough to be heard by the servants. I was shown out like some damned impertinent tradesman."

"Which had you so furious you retreated to your club for liquid luncheon and sympathy?" Petteril suggested.

An unhappy smile curved Austen's lips. "Something like that. I might have complained to one or two people. I certainly knocked back enough to fall asleep almost as soon as I got home and collapsed on the sofa."

"When was that?" Lord Petteril enquired.

Austen shrugged. "Around ten, according to Jackson—the butler—who let me in."

"And when did you wake?"

Austen grimaced. "About three in the morning. Hislop, my valet, had thrown a blanket over me and left me to it."

"What time did he do that?" Petteril asked.

"Before eleven."

"Which still gives you time to get to Kensington by midnight."

"I didn't! Kensington was the last place I wanted to be! Ever!"

"How did your pistol get there?"

The colour faded from Austen's face. "I don't know," he said stiffly.

He's lying. April peered at him. It wasn't quite defiance she read in his face. She didn't know him well enough to tell what it was. Nobs were pretty-well incomprehensible anyway.

"Was it stolen from you?" Petteril asked.

"It must have been," Austen said.

"By Mrs. Eastleigh?" Petteril hazarded, and April bestowed an approving look upon him.

Austen, however, glared. "No. She is not that kind of a woman."

Petteril did not press it. "When did you last see it?"

"Lord, I don't know. Years ago."

Oddly, that sounded truthful, spoken quickly and without thought.

"How many years?" Petteril asked.

"Two? Give or take a month or so."

"What does it look like?"

"A duelling pistol. Handsome, silver mounted."

Petteril frowned. "Do you still have the other?"

"Yes, I'll show it to you if you like."

"Don't trouble. I'll take your word for it. Why would someone steal a single duelling pistol?"

"To kill someone apparently," Austen snapped. "And implicate *me*!"

Petteril sat back. "Who do you think did such a thing? Who hates you that much?"

Austen and Haggard both stared at him, nonplussed.

"Don't have to hate *him*," April offered, looking up from her writing. "Just throw the blame off theirself."

"True," Lord Petteril allowed. "But how did the magistrate or his constables know it was your pistol?"

"Lord Dilworth recognized it," Austen said bleakly. "He's Barret's older brother, the Earl of Kinsley's heir. He'd seen me showing the pistols off at Manton's shooting gallery, years ago. Tried to buy them from me, actually. I refused, but they must have stuck in his mind. I wish it hadn't been him..." He shrugged impatiently. "And of course, when the constables came, I had only one pistol to show them. I had to admit the weapon used to kill Barret Bootle was mine."

"What did Mrs. Eastleigh say about it?" Petteril asked.

Austen blinked. "That she'd never seen it before in her life."

"Is that true?"

"So far as I can recall," Austen said steadily.

You're lying again. April noted his denial and added a large L beside it. *Why lie to your friends who're trying to get you off?*

The door beside April opened and a middle-aged lady wandered in. Her hair was not quite escaping from its pins, though there was an indefinable air of vagueness about her. She was very well dressed, though, walking with an expensive rustle through a haze of light and pleasant scent. April wanted her soap.

The gentlemen all sprang to their feet, though Austen looked annoyed. This must be the Aunt Moll his sister was supposed to have kept away.

"Goodness!" Aunt Moll exclaimed. "I did not know you had callers, Percy. How agreeable!"

Mr. Austen said loudly, "Aunt Molly, these are my old friends from university days, Lord Petteril and Sir Peter Haggard. Gentlemen, my aunt, Mrs. Manners."

The men bowed.

"How do you do, Mrs. Manners?" Sir Peter murmured.

"That's right, sir, you did dance with my niece!" Mrs. Manners beamed from him to Lord Petteril. "You both danced with Louise. I'll send for her, and tea..."

"No, no, Aunt, my friends are just leaving," Austen protested.

"I beg your pardon?" said Mrs. Manners.

"She's deaf as a post," Austen muttered and tried again more loudly. "They have to go!"

"There's no need to be rude, Percy."

A strangled snort emanated from Lord Petteril's direction, but fortunately, Miss Austen swept into the room at that point.

"There you are, Aunt!" she exclaimed, taking the older lady's arm. "Tea is served in the drawing room. Gentlemen, will you join us?"

"They are just leaving," Mrs. Manners said, with a gracious smile over her shoulder to the gentlemen. "Goodbye!" Facing forward once more, she caught sight of April and blinked. Miss Austen, who was unexpectedly pretty up-close, with a heart-shaped face and humorous eyes, cast her a quick, clear glance. April met it with equal curiosity, and her heart sank. Which made her angry.

Chapter Two

"'Ere," April said to Piers as she stalked out of the house beside him. "I thought you never danced?"

"That aunt," Piers said, "is only manipulatively deaf."

"What does that mean?" April demanded.

Piers ignored her and climbed into the waiting carriage.

"It means he was almost shamed into dancing," Haggard said, clearly amused. "But not quite. In you go."

"Where are we going now?" April asked, plonking down on the bench. "To see this Mrs. Eastleigh?"

"I think we should first give our condolences to Lord Kinsley," Piers said.

"Do you know him?" Haggard asked, surprised.

"Lord, no. But I *might* have been acquainted his late son. He doesn't know that I wasn't. And I expect you were."

"*I* wasn't," April said, as the horses moved forward. "And you can't take *me* into an earl's drawing room. I'll flim-flam the servants."

"Good girl," Piers approved.

"I could find an excuse to speak to theirs and all," April added, jerking her head back at the Austens' house. "Tomorrow, maybe." She frowned, grabbing onto the bench as the carriage bounced over the cobbles. "You know he's lying, right? About the pistol?"

So she thought so, too. He had been right to bring her.

Not quite so pleased, Haggard said, "What in particular about the pistol do you believe he is lying about?"

"About not knowing how it got to Mrs. Eastleigh's house. And about her never seeing it before." April wrinkled her nose. "Or at least about him *knowing* she hasn't seen it before. He might be protecting her. Or thinks he is."

"Sounds like Austen," Haggs said ruefully.

"And doesn't make our task any easier," Piers said. "Well, we shall have to find proof without him." His eyes focused on April. "If they let you into the kitchen, you'd best imply you're accompanying my aunt or cousin. Or waiting for her."

Haggs regarded him with some fascination. "Such deceit," he marvelled.

"You seen nothing yet, mister," April muttered.

"Be silent, child or you shall have no supper," Piers said flippantly. He didn't want to think of his role playing as deceit, though he supposed that was what it was. And to inflict it upon a grieving family was hardly compassionate or gentlemanly.

His unease increased as they were shown into the house of mourning. He had faced too much grief of his own in recent years to be comfortable around other people's. It was Haggs who spoke to the servant at the door, saying they had come to pay their condolences to Lord and Lady Kinsley, while Piers merely dropped his card on the silver tray provided.

They were welcomed by Lady Kinsley who, ramrod straight and unsmiling, did not wear her emotions on her sleeve. She accepted their condolences graciously as her due and invited them to be seated. Two grave ladies, who had clearly called upon the same task, took their leave.

Piers found himself sitting beside a middle-aged gentleman who looked more angry than sorrowful. If this was Lord Kinsley, Piers did not blame him. It was a terrible, pointless way to lose a son.

"Petteril, eh?" this gentleman barked at him. "I knew your uncle."

Piers said nothing, merely nodded and tried to give off a sympathetic silence. Since Haggard had his back to him, talking to a younger man, Piers had no way of knowing if this was the earl or not. He had no desire to put his foot in it.

The older man's brows twitched. "Didn't know you were a friend of my son's."

Relieved, Piers said, "Our acquaintance was not of long-standing. But I was so shocked when Haggard told me of his—"

"Shocked! I should say so! It is a disgraceful, disgusting crime. In my day, gentlemen took their quarrels outside to a meeting between equals, with all honour respected. They did not shoot each other in the head over lightskirts!"

"Perhaps it was not a gentleman who did it," Piers suggested.

Kinsley stared at him. "Don't be ridiculous. Plain as the nose on your face. The gun was Austen's. He admits it! Man probably still has a key to the damned house."

"Papa," said the younger man warningly. He had risen as a woman came towards them. She was perhaps four or five and thirty years, wearing widow's weeds. Black did not suit her, but her willowy figure was fashionable, and there was beauty in the shapely bones of her face.

Piers rose at once.

"Mrs. Bootle," Haggard said, bowing. "My profound condolences."

"Thank you, Sir Peter. You are very kind," the widow replied in little more than a whisper.

Haggard said, "I think you are not acquainted with my friend, Lord Petteril?"

"I am so sorry," Petteril told her. What else could he say to a woman who had not only lost her husband but faced the humiliation of his dying in the house of his mistress?

Despite her apparent frailty, she met his gaze with an unexpected challenge. "Did I overhear you correctly, my lord? You do not believe Mr. Austen killed my husband?"

"Barbara, don't upset yourself by dwelling on the subject," Kinsley said awkwardly.

She stared at him. "For God's sake, sir, how can I dwell upon anything else? My husband was murdered."

"By Austen. Let the law take its course."

"Well, if it was not Austen, I know *exactly* who it was," she said shakily, and yet with a malevolent flash of her eyes. "That Woman."

Her tone gave the words capital letters, like a title. And Mrs. Eastleigh was certainly a more likely suspect than Percy Austen. If she *had* done it, it would also explain Percy's lies about the gun. He had always been chivalrous by nature and it would be just like him to protect her, even from so heinous a crime. Piers imagined she could easily have stolen it from him before they parted.

"Not a woman's crime," Kinsley said awkwardly.

"Nor a gentleman's," the younger man snapped, "but it was sure as heaven one of them and my money's on the Eastleigh woman. I suggest we leave the debate to the law." He turned his amiable yet implacable gaze upon Piers. "We've never met, Petteril. I'm Dilworth."

Elder brother of the dead man and Kinsley's heir. Piers shook the proffered hand. "My condolences. If there is any way at all I can help, please let me know."

"You are kind," the widow said bitterly. "But it is beyond the ability of man to bring my husband back."

There was a limit to how much prying one could do during such a call, and in any case, Piers felt the hairs on the back of his neck standing up. They did not stay beyond another five minutes, and as soon as the door closed behind them, Piers let out his breath in relief.

"Sorry," Haggard said awkwardly. "Brings it all back, I suspect. Other people's grief. With me, too."

Piers inhaled, clapped him on the shoulder, and strode into the carriage. April bolted up the area steps a moment later and threw herself down opposite them.

"Did you see any?" Piers asked as the carriage edged forward into Hanover Square.

"Any what?" Haggard asked.

"Grief."

Haggard frowned at him.

April just looked at him thoughtfully. "Did you?"

"I saw anger, outrage, resentment, even fear. Jealousy on the part of the widow. All understandable. But no grief. Does no one *miss* the man?" He blinked and waved one dismissive hand. "I expect they're still shocked. Everyone grieves in their own way, and we are strangers. And yet..."

"It is worth considering," Haggard allowed. "Shall we go home?"

"No," Piers said decisively. "Let's go to Kensington and see if the ladybird grieves."

April, who was frowning over something, asked suddenly, "What happened to the husband? Mr. Eastleigh?"

"I doubt there ever was a Mr. Eastleigh," Haggs said. "It's merely a convention, to give the lady the outward respectability of a widow living alone. Mostly."

April curled her lip. "You lot got conventions for everything. Even cheating your wives."

"Valid point," Piers murmured. "We do like a certain order in our irregularities."

She glared at him, as though suspecting levity. "You got a respectable widow stashed somewhere, too?"

"No," Piers said. "And don't go asking Sir Peter or anyone else the same question."

"That a convention, too?" she asked with scorn.

"Yes."

"Gawd's bottom," she muttered.

Haggs laughed.

The carriage took them past Hyde Park and on to Kensington, to the neat little house occupied by Mrs. Eastleigh. It was a quiet, respectable street, the kind of place, apparently, where wealthy men hid their peccadillos.

"Have you been here before?" Piers asked Haggard.

"No. Are you thinking she won't admit us? Send in the cards," Haggard said cynically. "She'll receive any old viscount and baronet."

It was true that the lady was—probably—without a protector now, yet to assume such cynical greed made Piers uncomfortable. Especially under April's unforgiving stare. She didn't judge by the accepted morality of society. But it seemed Haggard was right, for the maid barely glanced at the cards before showing them straight into Mrs. Eastleigh's parlour. April slipped in after them.

"I know your names," said a rather lovely young woman, still in her twenties, advancing straight toward them. A riot of reddish-blonde curls was styled in artful disarray. Her gown was black silk and modest, though embroidered with jet beads and trimmed with intricate lace. Mourning suited her much better than it did the widow. "Percy spoke of you often. Please, come and—" She broke off as her gaze stumbled on April and fixed. Her brow twitched.

Piers was about to explain when he realized April was also staring at Mrs. Eastleigh, her eyes round as saucers.

"*Annie?*" she blurted.

April couldn't believe her eyes.

Mrs. Eastleigh was Annie from the Queen's Head, Annie who had always been kind to her, even when she knew her secret and had kept it. But it had been two years, maybe even three since Annie had left St. Giles for her new life. And she had never seen April in skirts. It was no wonder Annie didn't recognize her.

Or want to? After all, the few words Annie had said had been in a very refined accent.

"Sorry," April mumbled, stepping back, but Annie moved too, peering at her between the two men.

"Ape?" she asked doubtfully, and then when April grinned, so did she. "Ape, you little monkey! What the devil are you doing here?"

Annie dragged her forward and into a bear-hug.

April bore it. She might even have bestowed the tiniest hug in response before breaking free. "I come with them," she said jerking her head to Lord Petteril and Sir Peter who were regarding the scene with some interest.

Annie swung around to them, scowling, her hands on her hips. "Oh, yes? And what's my Ape to you two fine gentlemen?" she demanded, her eyes kindling.

"Um, your accent slipped," Lord Petteril said mildly.

Annie's expression was almost ludicrous. Annoyance that she had forgotten, fear that it would somehow land her in difficulties, and somewhere, still, a determination to protect Ape.

April tugged at her arm. "Don't be daft. I work for him, and he don't judge me, so he ain't judging you. Are you, mister?"

"Absolutely not," Lord Petteril said meekly. "Nor is Sir Peter." He held out his hand. "I'm Petteril, and glad to meet someone who has been a friend to April. Mrs. Eastleigh, I presume?"

Annie, though clearly still suspicious, found herself curtseying and taking the outstretched hand, although she cast an almost desperate glance at April, as though for guidance.

"Yes, I'm Mrs. Eastleigh," she said, flushing. "How can I help you? Did Percy ask you to call?"

"He didn't forbid it," Haggard murmured.

"His lordship here is quite good at solving puzzles," April said. "He's a clever cove. So we thought we'd try and work out what happened to this friend of yours that got killed here."

As though just remembering again, Annie groaned and sank down onto the nearest chair, waving the others to be seated also.

"The law thinks it's Percy," Annie said desperately, "but it isn't. Percy is the gentlest of men and wouldn't hurt a fly." She frowned. "Well, he might punch someone in a fit of temper, but dear God, he wouldn't come back in the dead of night and blow his brains out!"

"No, that isn't at all like the man I remember," Petteril agreed. "How do you account for his pistol being here and used to murder Mr. Bootle?"

Annie's breath caught. "I can't," she said defiantly.

April would have thought it a lie, except Annie didn't lie to friends.

Petteril smiled faintly. "It would help a great deal if you could."

"Look, the gun might be his, but he didn't fire it," Annie insisted.

"Did you?" Petteril asked steadily.

Annie sprang to her feet. "I thought you said he was a friend?" she threw at April.

"He is, so you've no cause to lie to him," April muttered, yanking Annie back down beside her. "Look, if he hurt you, if you had to defend yourself, we'll just get you out of here, won't we mister? I mean, my lord."

"April!" Haggard objected. "You can't commit his lordship to that."

"I have every sympathy with females forced to defend themselves," Lord Petteril said. "But I need to know the truth. *Did* you have to defend yourself?"

Annie opened her mouth, then slumped back in here chair. "No. I didn't shoot him and neither did Percy."

"Then who did? That young girl who showed us in?"

"Good God, no," Annie said, appalled.

"Then who do you think did it?"

Annie grimaced. "Could have been his wife, vinegary old thing, except I doubt she'd know where Kensington is. More likely his brother. They fought like cat and dog."

"Lord Dilworth?" Petteril said with interest.

"That's him. Barret called him Toby, but he's the old man's heir which gives him the courtesy title. He thought it also meant he could boss Barret around but Barret always dug his heels in on principal.

Nasty piece of work, Toby Dilworth. He came here once, you know, tried to buy me off."

"Why?" Petteril asked. "None of his business, was it?"

"No. Expect Barbara, Barret's wife, put him up to it. She was desperate for a baby and thought he wasted all his time with other women."

"Hmm." Petteril leaned forward in his chair. "So, tell me about the quarrel between Percy and Bootle earlier in the day. Did you witness it?"

"Yes," she said reluctantly. "Barret had no call to speak to Percy like that, and so I told him. I wouldn't have blamed Percy for thumping him, but then he wouldn't do such a thing in front of me. Always treated me like a lady, Percy did."

"Did Mr. Bootle treat you like a lady?" Petteril asked innocently.

Annie regarded him with unexpected humour. "Yes, but he wasn't so naïve. I never had to pretend with Barret. He didn't mind what I was." She blinked rapidly, and April knew that she had cared for him. But then, Annie would. Her throat closed up in sudden pity.

Lord Petteril only gave her a moment. "What happened that night? Where was Barret Bootle when he was shot?"

Annie stood up. "I'll show you if you like."

With Annie leading the way, they all trooped out of the parlour and across the passage to another cosy, much more masculine room with comfortable leather chairs by the fireplace, a mahogany desk with drawers under the window, paintings of hunting and battle scenes on the walls, and decanters and glasses on a rather fine table.

Annie sailed into the room and then stopped dead. April could almost feel the memory hitting her like an unexpected blow. Annie had grown up in St. Giles. She was used to violence and death. And yet...

April touched her fingers and Annie gripped hard for a moment before letting her go.

"He was sitting in that chair," Annie said, pointing not quite steadily at the armchair to the left of the fireplace.

"And shot in the back of the head," Lord Petteril murmured, walking over to the chair. He moved behind it and glanced at the window and then the doorway. He sat in the chair, which showed no signs of the recent violence, and sat forward to peer round at the door. "Was the window open?" he asked Annie.

"No. Locked and unbroken. And the doors weren't damaged either, which is why they seem to think Percy came in with his key. Only, he doesn't have one. He gave it to me when we parted." She shrugged. "But we can't prove that."

"Anyone could have dubbed the jigger," April said.

"What?" Sir Peter asked, baffled.

"Picked the lock on the door—front or back," April said impatiently. "If his nibs was sitting there, he'd not even see him come in. Probably thought it was Annie."

Lord Petteril stood up rather quickly. "Do you have servants who live in?"

"Just my maid, Jenny, the girl you saw already. There's a cook comes in daily and a woman who cleans three times a week, but they don't live here."

"So did you or Jenny hear or see anything odd that evening?" Petteril asked.

Annie shuddered. "What, apart from a gunshot that made me jump almost through the roof? And the sight of—" She broke off, catching Lord Petteril's eyes, and drew a deep breath. "No," she said almost humbly, and April had to smother a smile. There was something about his lordship that disarmed anger and self-pity.

"Austen said the shot came around midnight?" he said.

"About that. I was upstairs, getting ready for bed. Jenny was with me."

"When was the last time you saw Mr. Bootle alive? Where was he then?"

"We came out of the parlour together, then he came in here for a glass of brandy while I went upstairs. Must have been about half past eleven."

"No visitors that evening? That you know of?"

"No, we were quiet. Think Barret liked the peace, to be honest. At home, he'd get dragged around to parties and balls and theatre, and he couldn't always be bothered. I let him be." She blinked rapidly. "Sometimes, he even fell asleep in here by himself and came up to bed in the middle of the night."

So he might even have fallen asleep when his assailant sneaked in and shot him in the back of his head...

"How'd he get out?" April asked. "The murderer?"

Annie flapped one arm. "By the front door. It was wide open when Jenny and me rushed downstairs with the poker. He'd already gone, and Barret was dead. Jenny went out and yelled like a banshee for the Watch. Can we go back to the parlour now?"

"Of course..." Petteril said apologetically, then, "Wait, where was the pistol when you came in?"

"There, just where Ape's standing beside the chair."

April stepped instinctively out of the way and scowled at Petteril. "Why? You're not thinking he did it himself, are you?"

"Not if he was shot in the back of the head, no... Just trying to see what happened. The murderer could have brought the pistol with him and dropped it deliberately to incriminate Austen." He looked at Annie. "Who hates Austen?"

"No one that I know of. Barret wasn't too keen on him, but that was jealousy, and he sure as hell didn't shoot himself to spite Percy." She stomped off out of the room and everyone else followed her back to the parlour.

"It couldn't have been a passing burglar, could it?" Haggard said. "If Austen had left the pistol here, it could have been sitting on the table. Bootle could even have been examining it, when the burglar snatched it from him and shot him."

"He was still sitting in the chair when I found him," Annie protested. "Just with his head bowed, like he was sleeping..."

"Besides, burglars don't go about murdering people," April said severely. "Was anything prigged, Annie?"

Annie shook her head. "No," she said, though there was uncertainty in her voice.

"What?" April pounced.

"He only had one sleeve button when we found him. I never found the other."

"He could have dropped that anywhere," Petteril pointed out.

Annie nodded. "He could, and I can't swear he didn't have it when he came that evening, but I think I'd have noticed. It's certainly not here, and I tore the place apart cleaning it." She sniffed and glanced from April to Lord Petteril. "Do you think it's important? I told the magistrate but he didn't seem interested."

Petteril stirred. "What were they like, these sleeve buttons?"

"Gold, with his initials engraved on the front. *BB*. The right one was missing. Only the right one had my name on the other side.

Anne, inside a heart formed from the tail of the *A*. His family never found it, did they?"

"We can ask," April said briskly, although she wasn't sure how. She just knew that it meant a lot to Annie to have it back.

Sir Peter Haggard was still contemplating the burglar for he said, "What if Bootle threatened someone who broke in? Wouldn't a burglar shoot to protect himself?"

"Maybe," April said doubtfully. "More likely to bolt, but I suppose if he couldn't..."

"Except there was no struggle," Petteril pointed out. "And surely Bootle would not be playing about with a loaded duelling pistol. Or even leave it on a table where anyone could pick it up. These things go off if you breathe on them."

"Slight exaggeration, but I take your point," Haggard said with a sigh.

"Bit lethal for someone to be carrying it through the streets then," April observed. "Or standing in the house loading it before he shot the cove. Sorry, Annie."

Anne cast her a quick, distracted smile of forgiveness.

"No, you're right about one thing, though, Haggs. I think the pistol was here." Lord Petteril gazed at Annie. "It really would help to know the truth. Was it here?"

"Makes no difference," Annie muttered, throwing herself onto the sofa. "I'll never say to the beak that it was."

Petteril held her gaze, then, rather to April's surprise, his lips quirked into something close to a smile. As if he understood. Then he stretched his back and said, "It's enough to start with. Sorry to upset you, Mrs. Eastleigh. We'll take our leave."

Annie blinked at him, cast a quick, quizzical glance at April, then rose and curtsied. "My lord," she said primly, and to Haggard, "Sir."

"D'you want me to stay tonight?" April asked. "I can sleep in here. Or anywhere, really."

Annie threw her arms round her again. "Bless you, Ape, there's no need. I got Jenny. You go home with him, if he's treating you right. He *seems* like a gentleman."

Petteril waved his hat on his way out the door.

April extracted herself, unhappy that she wasn't needed and disliking herself for it. For years, Annie had been both a heroine and a symbol of hope, a proof that you could get out of St. Giles and the interminable dirt and poverty. She had never truly expected to see Annie again, and yet now that she had, everything had changed.

"Come back tomorrow and we can talk properly," Annie muttered with a quick glance at the door. "Can you?"

"Sure." April swaggered out the door, very much like Ape.

Chapter Three

Anne Eastleigh was sitting in her parlour thinking about Ape and the oddity of his—*her*—situation, when she realized how gloomy the evening had grown. The mist had not quite lifted and it made everything darker than usual. However, she hesitated to light the candles. Now that Barret was dead, she would have to make them last...

She shivered as if someone "walked over her grave" and abruptly, she rose and lit all the candles in the room. Just for five minutes, and then she would blow them out and go to bed...

Before she had even sat down again, she heard the knock at the door and tensed. Who would call at this time of night?

Percy?

She suspected Percy would be keeping his distance in case he implicated her in conspiracy. He was a dear, Percy. In many ways dearer than Barret, though she still thought of him as boy while Barret had always been grown up and manly...

Jenny pushed open the door, looking both awed and frightened. "Mrs. Bootle is here, ma'am! Will I say you're in bed?"

Annie gripped the back of the nearest chair. "Is she alone?"

"Yes, ma'am."

"Then you'd better show her in. And wait where you can hear me shout for you," she added grimly.

As Jenny scuttled away to obey, Annie threw her shoulders back and thought of all the truly frightening people she knew. Barret's wife, she could eat for breakfast if she chose. She didn't.

Barbara Bootle was not really vinegar-faced as Barret had described his wife. She entered wearing unrelieved black and a thick veil, which she lifted only when Jenny had shut the parlour door. She wore a stern expression, her well-shaped mouth discontented, her eyes hard as she looked down her long nose at Annie. Actually, she was rather pretty, if ramrod stiff.

Annie stood equally as straight. "Mrs. Bootle?"

"Mrs. Eastleigh," said Barret's wife by way of an answer.

"How might I be of assistance?"

Percy had taught Annie to speak and behave like a lady. She knew it slipped occasionally, but she was still pretty good at it now. She could see the surprise in Mrs. Bootle's eyes.

"I wanted to look you in the eyes," Mrs. Bootle said. "Just once. I thought I would see there whether or not you murdered my husband."

Anne smiled coldly. "Thank you for according me the same opportunity."

The lady's eyes widened. After a moment, she said, "You really believe I could have done that, don't you? I assure you, I was not born in the gutter!"

At least she didn't add *like you*, but Annie laughed anyway. "My dear lady, noblemen —and women—are as capable of murder as anyone else. They just have less reason, never being short."

"And did my husband keep you short, Mrs. Eastleigh?"

"No, he was excessively generous," Annie said, not entirely truthfully. "But I don't imagine you missed out on the housekeeping money."

"I don't know what you mean," Mrs. Bootle said grandly. Her gloved fingers were linked in front of her, gripping each other hard, and with a sudden surge of pity, Annie guessed something of the courage it had cost the other woman to come here. She doubted Barret's wife had loved him very much, but she probably did miss him, and the place of his death had undeniably humiliated her.

"I did not kill him, Mrs. Bootle," she said steadily.

The other woman stared at her, then abruptly turned on her heel. "Then it must have been Percy Austen after all."

"It was not," Annie said, starting forward, but Mrs. Bootle moved with surprising speed.

"Good night, Mrs. Eastleigh," she said, without turning, and walked out. If she saw Jenny skulking in the passage she gave no sign of it, merely sailed on out of the front door.

Petteril House was a much pleasanter place to be than when April had first come here, when there had been no servants, just oppressive, dark rooms and a general atmosphere of death and misery. Now, fully staffed and mostly redecorated, the house was bright and polished, the rooms gracious and light, even the library with its dark wood tables and bookshelves.

It was in this pleasant library that Lord Petteril resumed the reading and writing lessons he had begun in March before going down to Haybury Court.

April and Benson the groom, who had accompanied him to the country, were more advanced now, and left largely to read and write by themselves.

When the other students had gone, April gathered up the books and slates and said, "What you going to do today then?"

"Get Percy's servants to confirm or not when he came home the night Bootle died, and if he could have gone out again. Also, when any of them last saw the pistol in question. I might see if I talk to the medical examiner, too, make sure Bootle's wounds are where Percy said, and if he has any insight." He glanced round from the window. "Did you learn anything from Kinsley's servants?"

"Just that they don't seem that content considering they're working for an earl. Don't seem a very happy house to me."

"Well, one of the family has been murdered."

"Before that! I overheard a few remarks about quarrels and women—well we know Barret wasn't faithful to his wife, because he had Annie." She paused, wondering suddenly how she would feel in Mrs. Bootle's position. And then in Annie's. "Gawd, who'd have a man?"

Lord Petteril grunted. "Wrong person to ask."

"If you was leg-shackled, would you be faithful to your wife, or would you have an Annie?"

He blinked. "I suspect that would depend on both women concerned. And since neither applies to me at the moment—"

He didn't appear angry, so she almost interrupted with another question. But since the idea of him being married to anyone appalled her for any number of reasons she didn't want to think about, she merely said, "I'll go and see Annie, then, if you're doing the servants."

He nodded, apparently distracted by other thoughts, and she was halfway to the door before he said, "April? Be careful."

She half-turned and met his gaze. She scowled. "Annie didn't kill Barret Bootle."

"Someone did, and she's lying about the pistol."

"Not for the reasons you think," April said stoutly.

"Just be careful." He opened a drawer and threw her a purse. "Take a hackney there and back."

She obeyed, since walking would take too long, but from the suspicion and care learned on the docks and in St. Giles, she got the hackney to drop her in the street before Annie's and walked the rest of the way.

Which was how she came to notice the carriage travelling very slowly along Annie's quiet road. April walked fast, as she always did, and she caught up easily with the carriage. She cast a casual look to the side through the window, but she needn't have worried about being seen. The sole occupant of the carriage had his gaze fixed somewhere beyond her. Even so, fear clawed at her stomach because the man in the carriage looked very much like Jason Marr.

Captain Jace as he liked to be known. This cove had the same thick, dirty-fair hair, the same long side whiskers, and the same tall beaver hat with the large brass buckle that he told everyone was gold.

And when she followed the direction of his gaze, she saw with fresh alarm that it was Annie's house he was watching so carefully.

April was so appalled she walked straight past Annie's place and around the corner, where she waited, skulking, for Marr's carriage to pass—which it did at a suddenly fast clip, heading eastward, no doubt back to St. Giles and the Queen's Head which was his chief brothel and headquarters of his nasty little empire.

April wiped her sweating palms on her skirts as she walked more slowly back to Annie's house. Petteril's warning rang in her ears. She knew damned well to be careful of Captain Jace Marr, but did she need to be careful of Annie too? Or was it Annie who needed to be careful? Why was Jace watching her house? Had Annie never truly left Jace's protection?

Or was she working *with* him? Had they killed Barret Bootle between them?

April flushed with shame. She refused to think such a thing of Annie. For one thing, there was genuine grief in her old friend for her lover. For another, Annie's basic kindness surely ruled out such a crime. Not that she would be incapable of knifing someone who threatened her or a friend. But to ally with Marr to cold-bloodedly shoot her generous lover? No, that was not Annie. She was more likely to croak Marr himself, however scared of him she was.

Still, if Jace was involved, April's nerves shrieked to warn Lord Petteril immediately.

Instead, she walked up the little path, knocked on Annie's door and was admitted by the cheerful young maid, Jenny, who recognized her from last night.

Jenny showed her into a cosy dining room, where Annie was sitting at the table, a cup of tea in one hand, a plate of ham and eggs in front of her. She sprang up with clear delight at the sight of April.

"Ape! Come and sit down. Have some breakfast!"

"Oh, no, I had mine hours ago," April replied. "I'll have a cup of tea, though."

Jenny put a cup and saucer in front of her and Annie poured tea into it.

"Tell me everything," Annie said, picking up her fork. "How'd you come to be working for this fancy lord? Do you live in his house?"

April nodded. "Yes." In St. Giles, Annie, older and wiser and basically kind, had been her closest thing to a friend. Yet now, she found she didn't want to tell her how she had come to meet Lord Petteril. That was too...private. Even though it was also funny and might have made Annie laugh. "He thought I prigged something from him and I didn't, so I helped him find it and he let me work in his stable for a bit. Only he worked out I weren't a boy and made me wear skirts instead and be his assistant."

Annie smiled, looking her over. "You scrubbed up pretty well, Ape. You make a pretty girl, not just in the common way, either. Does *he* think so?"

They both knew who *he* was. April felt blood seep uncomfortably into her face. "Don't be daft. He don't look at me at all that way." And April most certainly didn't want to think about *that.*

Annie looked sceptical. "You sure?"

"Quite sure!" April snapped, glaring. "Skirts or trousers, I'm just Ape to him."

Annie was watching her very carefully. "He calls you April. Is he kind?"

This was simpler ground, which April welcomed with relief. "Oh yes. Taught me to read and write. Not just me," she added, catching something in Annie's expression. "He teaches any of his servants who want to, just like being in school. He was a teacher at university before he got the title and everything, so he's good at it." She took a large mouthful of tea and set down her cup, holding Annie's eyes. "He'll find out who killed your Mr. Bootle."

"Just to prove it wasn't his friend."

"Yes, but also for the truth. He don't like people croaking." She almost asked her about Jace, then, but was afraid it would make Annie clam up. Too much time had passed. Annie had no reason to trust her still. "Must be horrible for you. The beak thinking one of your gents did in the other."

Annie smiled, memory and sorrow in her face. "Oh, Percy weren't my gent anymore. I met him up Haymarket one night, like I told you three years ago when I got out of St. Giles. He were a real gentleman, even though he was so young. Gentle and kind, you know?"

In Annie's world, gentleness and kindness were rare enough. No wonder she'd been so taken with Percy Austen. "He gave me this house. I told you that, too. Never thought, sharing a room with all the other whores in the Queen's Head, that I'd have me own house."

"What happened? Why'd you and him part?"

Annie sighed. "Think he grew up. Novelty wore off, didn't it? Frolicking's all very well, but I ain't of his world and he ain't of mine. Took me to the theatre once or twice, but it was all pretty stuffy and he didn't like when I waved to the opera dancers I knew. You can only get so far out of St. Giles, Ape. This is as far as I get, but I'll take it."

"You're doing well, Annie," April assured her, while some other unease twisted inside her. April had got out of St. Giles too, thanks to Lord Petteril. In spite of everything, she thought of Petteril as her friend. But he wasn't. Like Annie said, you only got so far out of the slums. "How'd you meet this Barret Bootle, then?"

"Percy'd bring his friends here, sometimes. Young fellows mostly—though never your fancy lordship. I just knew of him and the other fellow, Sir Whatsit, from Percy's funny stories. When they were students, like. But Barret came once, and he were different." Annie smiled. "Older, more serious, you know? He weren't foxed like the others. Think he only came to play cards, but I had to put a stop to that 'cause Percy and the others were too jug-bitten and losing too much. Educated young gents can be just as bloody stupid as our lot."

"I know," April said, though she didn't really. "Did Barret mind that you stopped him fleecing 'em?"

"No, and I like him for that. But it made him notice me. And I could see he liked me. Percy must have told him we were parting ways, because he came to see me by himself after that—respectable, like—before he made me an offer. *Carte blanche*, the nobs call it. It's French. Anyway, Percy always meant to keep the lease on this for me—he'd promised me from the beginning—but Barret didn't like that, so he took it over."

Annie smiled. "He liked having a home of his own, even this little house which don't compare to that bloody great mansion in Hanover Square. He and his wife didn't have their own place. They lived with his parents and his brother and I think they both hated that."

April let the silence stretch a little before she asked casually, "So what happens to the house now?"

Annie wrinkled her nose. "I don't know. If Barret has a will, he might have provided for me. His family will fight it, though. She came to see me last night, his wife. To see if I shot her husband. I don't think she did it after all. Pity. I'd have liked it to be her. Probably the brother."

"Where could the brother have got the gun?"

Annie blinked as though she had forgotten about it. She waved one dismissive hand, and April sat forward, glaring at her.

"You can't just go on lying about it," she said. "You and Percy both! You're fogging it all up so we can't find who really done it. That what you want, Annie? Without the truth, they'll hang your Percy for it."

Annie whitened. "Don't say that, Ape," she whispered.

"Then tell me about the bleeding gun, 'cause Percy ain't saying nothing—must be to protect you. It was here all the time, wasn't it?"

Annie stared at her, swallowed, then nodded miserably. "He gave me it for protection, for the nights I stayed here alone."

"And Percy won't say that 'cause it might cast the blame on you," April said slowly. "And you ain't saying it because he must have known where it was and could have used it to shoot Barret."

"He didn't," Annie whispered.

April sat back. "Someone did. Someone else must have known where you kept it. Where *did* you keep it?"

After another slightly frustrating conversation with Percy Austen, Piers talked to the family servants, who had all been instructed to co-operate and who all bore out the time of his arrival home on the night of the murder, and the state he had been in.

"Was he angry?" Piers asked his valet, Hislop.

"Oh, no, my lord," the man returned, shocked. "Mr. Austen was never an aggressive drunk. He smiled when I threw the blanket over him at a quarter before eleven."

The butler had given the same story, that Austen had been amiably foxed when he'd weaved through the front door to the library.

"Did you check on him afterwards?" Piers asked Hislop. "Did you hear him going to bed?"

"No, my lord. No one did. But I found him in bed the next morning with a sore head."

"When was that?"

"At nine of the clock, sir."

Piers sighed. Basically, there was no one to account for Austen's presence between a quarter to eleven that night and nine the following morning. His own drunkenness accounted for it in Piers's mind, but he doubted that would impress a magistrate, let alone a judge and jury, not with Lord Kinsley baying for blood.

Running downstairs from Percy's dressing room, where he had interviewed the valet, Piers saw Miss Austen come out of the morning room and then wait for him. She had a pleasing, distinctive face that appealed to him as conventional beauty did not. He had recognized her easily yesterday, and, interestingly, he thought he would have done so even had she not been in Percy's company and in Percy's house.

She beckoned him into the morning room and he followed her, hoping she might be able to answer some of his questions.

"I don't suppose *you* heard Percy going to bed last Monday night?" he asked Louise without much hope.

"No," she said, immediately frowning with worry. "My aunt and I were at a ball and didn't come home until after three in the morning."

"You didn't happen to notice if Percy was in the library, did you?"

"I did look in there, but no, he wasn't."

"Then he must already have gone to bed." Though he would still have had time to go to Kensington, shoot Barret and go home to bed before three.

"I didn't look," Miss Austen said. "I fell into my own bed with some relief." She blushed under his gaze. "I find balls something of a trial, as you know."

"From my observation, you are enviably popular."

"That was only because you paid me attention," she said, her colour deepening further, which was intriguing. For the first time, it entered his head that Louise Austen liked him, for more than just being her brother's friend and someone who had, eventually, rescued her from a difficult social situation. Oddly, the thought was not displeasing. In fact, he found he was flattered.

He tried a smile, and she returned it with warmth. "It was Sir Peter who danced with you," he felt compelled to point out. "Though Lord knows why other gentlemen were so slow to notice you before that."

"Too much competition in the marriage mart," she said with distaste. "I prefer true friends to empty flatterers. My lord, is Percy in great trouble?"

"He won't be if we can only prove either that he was nowhere near the house in question at the time, or that somebody else committed the crime."

She looked startled. "How on earth do we do that?"

"Ask questions. Look into Mr. Bootle's life and find those who might have wished to end it and had the opportunity to do so."

"How..."

"Squalid?" he suggested. "Yes, I suppose it is, but it cannot be avoided if we are to prove Percy's innocence."

From rosily flushed, she turned pale. "I did not intend any criticism, my lord," she got out. "God knows I welcome your help in this. Percy will tell me nothing. I suppose the female in the house concerned is not respectable."

"Not in the least," Piers admitted. There was no point in lying.

"Is she accusing Percy?" Miss Austen asked with difficulty.

"Oh, no, quite the opposite. She insists on your brother's innocence, but she is hiding something. My assistant, April, has gone to see if she can get her to reveal it."

"Your assistant," Miss Austen repeated uncertainly. "The girl who was here with you and Sir Peter?"

"Indeed."

She searched his face for a moment, and Piers could not help being disappointed. He had hoped she would prove to be above such suspicions—though on so little knowledge she had no reason to be.

She turned away.

"Are you acquainted with Lord Dilworth?" he asked on impulse.

"The dead man's brother?" she said calmly, sitting by the low-burning fire. "Yes, a little. I have danced with him, too."

"Do you like him?"

Colour seeped back into her pale cheeks. "Yes, of course. He is perfectly amiable. People are, on the dance floor."

"I wouldn't know," he said blandly. "But I heard he and his brother were at constant outs with each other. I wondered if you might have any insight on that."

"Oh goodness. You don't think Dilworth killed his own brother?"

"I have no idea, but he would hardly be the first man to do so."

She shook her head helplessly. "I cannot say."

Something in her expression alerted him to her distress, though she tried to hide it.

"Is he a suitor of yours?" he asked gently.

She waved one hand in denial. "No, no, of course not. He—he has paid me some attentions, enough to make my aunt hope, but truthfully, there is no real possibility of such a match."

"Because you do not like him?"

She smiled, a real smile this time. "You are the only person, my lord, who would not assume it to be the other way around."

He laughed, and departed before he destroyed her good opinion.

Chapter Four

"She kept it in the desk drawer in that study where his nibs died," April said triumphantly almost as soon as she entered Piers's library that afternoon.

"Ah! Well done. I wish she had said so yesterday."

April sat down opposite him. "She wouldn't admit to seeing it in the house because she thought it would incriminate Percy further. She still likes him."

"Does she?" Piers asked at once, raising his eyebrows.

April scowled at him. "Not in that way. Friends, like. He got her out of St. Giles, gave her a chance, and she'll always remember that."

"And he looks after her, too, refusing to admit he gave her the pistol in the first place," Piers said ruefully. "What a pair. Was it loaded?"

"Lord, no. She don't really like guns. But there were powder and balls in the drawer with it. Suppose Barret could have loaded it himself some time before, and the murderer just made use of it. You learn anything new from Percy? Or the examiner?"

Piers shook his head. "No one can vouch for Percy being in his own house at midnight when Barret died. And the doctor tells me the wound was definitely in the back of his head. Ball's still in there. Killed him instantly. The doctor turned out his clothes, too, never found the sleeve button Annie says is missing."

"Any ideas?" April asked hopefully.

He cast her a lopsided smile. "Trying to think how I can discover where Lord Dilworth and Mrs. Bootle really were when Barret died. According to the magistrate, they had each been at different parties but just happened to meet up in the drawing room at Kinsley House just before the murder took place."

"Don't you believe 'em?"

"I don't *dis*believe them. It just sounds too dashed convenient. But if I enquire of either, they'll throw me out the house and I'll learn nothing."

"The servants will do the same to me," she said ruefully. "Though I can hang about their ken, maybe follow someone on their day off and ask."

"You might have to."

They fell into silence, both thinking. After a few moments, he noticed that her fingers were twisting together in her lap, and he lifted his gaze to her face. He liked her countenance, piquant and vital, her delicate bones oddly beautiful with the contrast of her upturned nose. As a boy she had looked cheeky and appealing. As a girl, she would break hearts. And that both hurt him and filled him with pride. And fear. Was this how parents felt?

No. Absolutely not.

"There's something else," she said abruptly, her eyes flying up and catching his observation.

"What?"

"When I was walking along the road to Annie's, I saw Captain Jace," she said in a rush.

"Is that bad?" he asked cautiously.

"It's terrible! Jace was her pimp. He owns the Queen's Head. You do remember the Queen's Head?"

"Vividly. What's he captain of?"

April curled her lips. "Nothing. He just likes the sound of it. But Jace is a nasty piece of work. Violent, greedy, unpredictable. He'll hurt his girls—cut them so they're too ugly and can't work no more, even do them in—rather than let them away with an extra penny for a hard night's work."

Piers's stomach twisted, not just at the nastiness of the tale, but that April should be so aware of it that she counted it part of life.

"Got his finger into lots of gristly pies," she continued, grimacing. "Including Lord's prigging. And Tatty's fencing. You re—"

"Yes, I remember them perfectly. And Tatty's brother with the garotte, though I'm happy to say I never met him."

"You should be happy. He works for Jace and all."

Piers forced his brain to think beyond the awfulness of her old life. Of the lives others were still forced to live. "Was this Jace visiting Annie?"

"Nah, he seemed to be watching her house. Driving slowly past. Maybe he was trying to frighten her. Or just see what she was up to. Or who with."

"Did you ask her about him?"

April shook her head, looking unusually sheepish, even awkward. "I couldn't. She was so busy telling me how she'd left St. Giles behind her, I couldn't bring myself to ask how come she ain't left Jace too."

His breath caught. "You think she hasn't? You think they were somehow together, maybe in squeezing money out of Barret? And Percy?"

Her knuckles were white. "Annie wouldn't. Not from choice. She liked 'em. She don't like Jace—she hid me from him more 'n once. He sells boys, too, you know. But he can make it hard to refuse. If he knows where she is, he can hurt her. In all sorts of ways. If she acted with him, she had no choice. And I don't know that she did."

"And you don't want her to think you don't trust her," he said gently. "Not if you're wrong."

She nodded, staring at her hands. "It'd solve everything if Jace did it."

He straightened. "Then let's see if we can find out where Jace was last Monday night when Bootle was shot."

She sprang up. "Oh, no! You ain't going to the Queen's Head asking questions about Jace! You'll get croaked!"

He considered. "I have the protection of Viscount Petteril, remember? And all the unpleasantness of the law to bring down on them." He was referring to an earlier visit to St. Giles in the guise of a forger with connections to Petteril.

"Won't do you no good when you're dead," she retorted. "Besides, no one ever gets Jace. There's a Bow Street Runner been after him for years. Never caught him yet. And I don't fancy our chances, neither. Only if we *can* pin it on a stranger, a villain, then Mr. Austen gets off."

"And Mr. Bootle has still been murdered."

She glared at him, clearly rattled about the prospect of his going to St. Giles and asking about this Jace. "Coves get murdered all the time." Colour crept under her skin and her eyes slid away. "It ain't right," she admitted. "But it happens."

In fact, he didn't fancy his chances of finding Captain Jace without her, and he certainly didn't want her in the man's line of fire. Another idea occurred. "What's this Runner's name?"

"The Runner?" she repeated, taken aback. She dropped back into her chair, frowning. "He asked me all sorts of questions once till I gave him the slip and had it away on my toes. What was his name? Something tangly..."

"Tangly?" he repeated.

She shook her head impatiently, then her frown cleared and she smiled up at him triumphantly. She really was breathtaking. "Knott! Jimmy Knott!"

A surge of laughter shook him. "Well done." He reached for a piece of paper.

"Why, what you going to do?" she asked suspiciously.

"Invite Mr. Knott to call upon me at his earliest convenience."

She gazed at him with considerable respect, to which he was far from immune. "Cor."

Joshua, the first footman, knocked on the open door to gain Piers's attention. "My lord, Captain Withan is here."

Cousin Bertie. What the devil did he want?

Money, of course. He had to ask for it now, rather than just help himself, which is what he and the rest of the family had been doing when Piers first came to take shaky possession of his inherited property. Piers had no desire whatever to see him.

He sighed. "Show him in," he said. Cousin Bertie, damn him, was his responsibility, too.

He was aware of April looking at him, looking for a sign as to whether she should stay or go. Deliberately, he didn't give her one, and then Bertie strutted in, in his smart, scarlet uniform.

"Well, Cousin?" he greeted Piers with gratingly false cheer. "I trust I find you in excellent health?"

"Thank you, yes," Piers replied, raising his quizzing glass at his visitor. "Not looking so good, yourself, Bertie. Not sick, are you?"

"No, just confoundedly bored," Bertie said unexpectedly.

His restless gaze skimmed over April, who knew enough to have stood up at the entrance of her better. Piers found himself tensing, for Bertie had a notoriously roving eye and he was exactly the sort who would consider servants fair game. And it was always possible he would recognize Ape the insolent stable lad.

But Bertie simply ignored her, returning his attention to Piers. He drew in his breath.

"Got a favour to ask, old boy."

Of course you have. How much? Piers waited, keeping his expression bland.

"I want to transfer to a fighting regiment. If you buy me a promotion, I can be on my way to the Peninsula this week."

Whatever Piers had expected, it was not that. Bertie, from his slightly rueful smile, had spotted his startlement.

"I could transfer easily at my present rank," he said, "but everyone would think I'd been disgraced, going straight from the Guards to the 23rd. With a commission as major, I'd be in a much better position."

Piers walked to the cabinet and poured two glasses of brandy, giving himself time to think. He gave one of the glasses to Bertie. "Bit sudden, isn't it?"

"Not really. I just forgot for a bit why I joined the army in the first place. And it wasn't to strut about Hyde Park or pretend to guard the King." Bertie raised his glass to his lips and swallowed convulsively. "Boredom makes me a bad man, Piers, you know that."

"And you'd rather be a good one?" he said politely.

Bertie's smile was twisted. "That's a stretch. I'd rather be a good soldier than waste my time. I'm thirty years old and I've never seen action."

"John saw action," Piers pointed out brutally, recalling their cousin who had died nearly two years ago at the first siege of Badajoz.

Bertie held his gaze. "I know. The profession comes with the risk as well as the glory. I have the chance of neither here. I'll be able to pay you back eventually—nothing to waste my money on in Spain, I imagine."

Bertie was serious. Behind the bravado and the half-humorous self-deprecation, there was even a hint of desperation. It was a place Piers had been, an antechamber to somewhere far worse, and he did not wish that on anyone, least of all a cousin who had shared his childhood. The last of his male cousins.

"I'm sure you'll find something," Piers said, and Bertie's eyes cleared with something like relief.

"Thanks, Piers," he said.

Piers clinked his glass against Bertie's and drank. When he lowered the glass, Bertie was extracting something from his pocket—a scrunched up card.

"From Aunt Hortensia," Bertie said. "She heard you were back in town and bade me deliver this. She's holding a ball tomorrow evening for Gussie. It can serve as a family farewell to me, too."

Piers would rather have said farewell here and now, but over Bertie's shoulder, his gaze met April's, and another thought occurred. "Does Aunt Hortensia know Lady Kinsley? Come to that, are you acquainted with her son, Dilworth?"

"They know each other pretty well, call each other friends, though I wouldn't say there was any *liking*. And I've been in a few scrapes with Dilworth. Why? They won't be at Gussie's ball—they're in mourning for the younger son who managed to get himself murdered."

"So I heard," Piers murmured. "What's Dilworth like?"

Bertie shrugged. "Decent enough fellow. They're a stuffy kind of family, but he was always reluctant to settle down. His brother married, while he avoided it and cut a dash about the town."

"Were the brothers friends?"

"God, no. Fought like cat and dog. Which doesn't mean he don't grieve."

"Do you know Mrs. Eastleigh?"

Bertie kissed the tips of his fingers. "Only sign of intelligence I saw in Barret Bootle."

"And Mrs. Bootle?"

"Stuffy as the rest of them. To be honest, I think Barret resented having settled down and rebelled. Why are you so interested in the Bootles?"

"No reason. I don't suppose you saw either of them last Monday evening?"

Bertie looked puzzled, and then amused. "No. No I didn't see any Bootles. I was in a gaming hell in Piccadilly." He smiled. "Didn't even play."

"Don't suppose you saw Percy Austen there, did you?" Piers asked with more flippancy than hope.

"I don't even know Percy Austen." Bertie finished his brandy. "Thanks for this, Piers. I won't forget it."

"Neither will I," Piers murmured as he strode off. "Though I will probably regret it."

"Nah," April said. "Be the making of him. You'll see."

Chapter Five

Jimmy Knott, the Bow Street Runner, presented himself at Petteril House at exactly nine in the morning—which was the hour of the staff reading lesson. Hastily giving each of his pupils a task to occupy them, Piers left the library and hurried downstairs to the reception room, where he had told Joshua to put the runner.

Inevitably, April followed.

"Mr. Knott," Piers greeted him. "I'm Petteril. Miss April here is my assistant."

Knott, looking like a man hiding his alarm, bowed low but rather stiffly. His gaze flickered over April and lingered, perhaps wondering why she looked familiar, then returned somewhat anxiously to Piers.

"How can I help your lordship?"

"Please, sit down," Piers invited, waving to one of the chairs by the fire. He took the other, while April perched by the little table at the window, where she opened her ubiquitous notebook. "I am interested in the movements of one Jason Marr, known, I believe, as Captain Jace."

Knott, who sat rigidly on the edge of his chair, stared at him. "How'd you even hear about the likes of him?"

"Oh, I hear lots of things," Piers said vaguely. "Among them that this Marr is a very dangerous individual whom you have tried for some time to...ah—incarcerate."

Knott looked gloomy. "Can't catch him in anything. Never any proof, and no one will speak against him, but I know he's done thieving and extortion and beatings. Even murder. But I can't catch the—"

"I appreciate the difficulty," Piers cut in. "Do you keep any kind of watch on him?"

"When I can. In my spare time. I got other thieves to take, in order to live. But I keep him under my eye when I can. Why? What's he to your lordship?"

"There was a murder in Kensington last Monday night. A Mr. Bootle was shot."

Knott nodded. "I heard about that. Shocking. A matter between gentlemen, I understand. Not Jace's lay at all."

"Are you sure? I understand Marr has many...interests."

Knott curled his lip. "Oh, he has. But not in Kensington."

April said, "What if one of his girls moved up in the world and went to live there?"

"She'd be daft to tell Jace where," Knott said.

"True," April said discontentedly.

"I don't suppose you happened to be watching Marr last Monday night?"

Knott scratched his head. "Actually, I was. He were in a tavern in St. Giles."

"The Queen's Head?" Piers hazarded.

"No, he goes elsewhere for recreation. The Ratter, down on Finnegan's Lane. People might talk there, but they don't do business. Strictly legal-like, though I don't care for their clientele. Jace was there Monday, drinking with Jerry Nash, Frankie Sullivan, Leeky and the rest."

"Leeky is Tatty's brother," April informed Piers, who couldn't prevent a hiss of laughter.

"He of the garrotte?"

"That's him," April replied. By the time she turned back to Knott, the runner's mouth had fallen open, gazing in astonishment from her to Piers and back. "When did Jace leave that night?" April asked.

Knott pulled himself back together. "Late. Nearly two o'clock when we was all told to go home. Jace and his cronies went out the back way. The rest of us used the front door like honest folks."

Piers leaned forward. "Was that the only time he left?"

"Yes. Sat glued to his seat for hours while others fetched him ale. Never even took off his hat."

"What, the tall one, with the buckle he thinks is gold?" April asked.

Knott's smile was half grimace. "That's the one. Like his best friend, that damned hat."

"He hides stuff under it. Opulent stuff and the likes."

Knott stared at her and blinked several times.

Piers stirred. "But sadly, it means he was not in Kensington at midnight last Monday, so he cannot be the man who killed Barret Bootle."

"Can't see any reason why he would," Knott said. "Unless he was paid, and that's so unlikely I shouldn't even think it. But one day I'll get the bastard for something." He coughed. "Begging your pardon, my lord, miss..."

It was a disappointment. Jace Marr, it seemed, was the only one of their suspects with an irreproachable alibi for the time in question. And you couldn't get a much better witness, than a Bow Street Runner, one of the magistrate's own men.

Percy Austen could not help feeling that every knock on the door heralded his arrest for Bootle's murder. With acute anxiety, he dwelled on the ruin such an arrest would bring to his sister, to his aunt and the rest of the family.

"Why don't we all go back to Dorset?" he blurted.

Louise met his gaze squarely, as she always did. "Because it will look like running away. Like guilt."

"I am guilty of nothing," he snapped.

"Then why do you not tell Lord Petteril the truth about the wretched pistol? Even if you don't tell me."

He tore his gaze free. "Because I already have. There is nothing more to tell."

There was silence, then. "Is this some kind of silly honour, Percy?"

"Honour is not silly."

"No, but *you* are. Lord Petteril is not the law. He is not even Lord Kinsley looking for someone to blame. He is your friend, and if he is to help you, he needs to know all the facts, even the ones that may not reflect well upon you."

She was right, of course. Damn her. He had told himself he had to keep the matter of the pistol secret, for Anne's sake. But Petteril would judge neither of them. Would he? He seemed willing enough to assume Percy's innocence, for old friendship if for no other reason. But Anne Eastleigh was nothing to him.

"Percy, this is serious," Louise said, such anxiety mingled with her frustration that he felt suddenly ashamed. Again.

"You are right," he said, rising from the chair which had grown suddenly so uncomfortable. "I'll go and see him now."

"I'll come with you," Louise said at once.

"You don't need to."

"Don't panic, Perce," she said wryly. "I shan't listen in to your conversation. I might search out his assistant instead."

He still looked uneasy. "You might not want to do that either," he said with difficulty.

But she only laughed at him. "If he is behaving improperly with the girl, he would hardly have brought her here to meet me and Aunt Moll, would he? Worry is impairing your judgement, Percy."

She was probably right. Again.

Since Aunt Molly was enjoying a nap before the evening's festivities, they ordered her carriage and drove over to Petteril House, which enjoyed a delightful corner position off Park Lane, which Percy suspected gave excellent views of the park.

Withy had certainly landed on his feet in one sense, inheriting the title and estate of Viscount Petteril against all the odds. On the other hand, Percy remembered Piers Withan as a rather determined academic and he doubted his old friend set much value on any of his inheritance. He had had to abandon his promising career at university and take up a role for which he was unsuited and untrained, and now he would be expected to marry and produce heirs.

Marry. For an instant, he focused on Louise. Louise did not really take to the London Season either. She was at once too critical and too humorous, and too fastidious to toady to the wealthy and the fashionable.

She liked Petteril, though. Percy could tell. And that was a marriage he would have no quarrel with at all. Although first, he would have to clear his own name. The pit of his stomach began to sting again.

They were shown immediately into Lord Petteril's library, where he and the girl April were drinking tea and arguing.

Withy, catching sight of Louise, sprang immediately to his feet.

Louise said, "Percy has something to tell you, my lord."

Percy glowered at her.

"Oh good," Piers said with a hint of humour. "But is it not teatime? We should repair to the drawing room."

"Perhaps," Louise said, "April could show me to the drawing room and you and Percy could join me when you have had your talk."

God preserve me from managing females, Percy thought with annoyance. Piers, however, looked more amused than anything. The girl, April, did not. But she only stuffed the book and pencil into the little bag she wore at her waist and led the way out of the library. Louise glared once over her shoulder at Percy, as though daring him not to tell what he had promised.

"Does it need brandy?" Withy asked.

Percy sighed. "No. No it needs a promise from you that what I say to you shall be confidential."

Piers's eyes remained steady. "If you need to ask, you should not tell me. I have done nothing to help you in any case."

Blood surged into Austen's face, burning. "I'm sorry, that was an unforgivable thing to say. Of course I do not doubt your discretion or your loyalty. How could I? It's just... I can't let Anne Eastleigh hang for this, and she would be a much more convenient scapegoat than I!"

"Sit," Piers commanded. "Talk."

Austen drew in his breath. "The pistol that killed Bootle was mine. But I gave it to Annie when we were together, just to be sure she was safe when I was not present."

Piers sat down. "I know."

Austen's jaw dropped. "You know? How?"

"April extracted it from Mrs. Eastleigh yesterday. Apparently, she was keeping the fact quiet in case it somehow implicated you. Not knowing, I presume, that you had already admitted the pistol was yours. Now, with honour satisfied, can we concentrate on the truth?"

"She would not have killed him, Withy. It's not in her nature."

Piers's dark eyes did not soften. "You do know her background?"

Austen lifted his chin. "She never tried to deny it."

"Survival in that world requires a steel you and I have never needed to acquire. On the other hand, I don't think she did do it. I think she was fond of Bootle and according to April, he never mistreated her."

Austen felt a muscle twitch at the corner of his eye. He didn't like that Anne was fond of Bootle. And he didn't like her cosiness with Withy's girl. He had never thought of himself as a dog-in-the-manger before.

"Your April," Austen said abruptly. "I presume she is of the same background."

Withy's eyes were opaque. "The background is similar. The foreground is not. And I insult neither of them by saying so. Shall we join Miss Austen for tea?"

In some subtle way, April sensed a threat from Miss Austen. Not because she was unpleasant or rude, or because she distrusted or disliked Lord Petteril. In fact, the opposites were true. Lord Petteril should one day marry a lady like Miss Austen—pretty, unconventional, and clever. And already half in love with him.

April hated the idea and wished she didn't.

"What a lovely room," Miss Austen said, when April showed her in.

"Lord Petteril had it redecorated," April offered. "It's much lighter and brighter now. He's doing the same to the country house in Haybury. Makes a difference, doesn't it?"

"I - I can't tell. I have never been in this room before."

April was unworthily pleased to have scored a point of familiarity if nothing else. Ashamed, she muttered, "I'll fetch the tea."

She forgot to curtsey of course, and when Miss Austen said, "Stay a moment," April assumed she was in trouble. She turned back, feeling the need to curtsey to no one except *him*.

Miss Austen smiled slightly, almost shyly, apparently not angry at all. "You have an interesting position for a woman."

"Interesting for anyone," April conceded. "I got lucky."

"How did that come about?"

"Oh, the usual way," replied April, who had no intention of ever telling anyone how she had met Lord Petteril.

But Miss Austen's eyes laughed at her. "I don't think that can possibly be true."

"It is," April insisted. "In the sense he offered me a place and I took it. I was down on my luck."

"And now it's all changed and you help him solve puzzles. What else do you do?"

"Organize parties, pretty up Haybury Court. Whatever he asks." She held the other woman's gaze. "And he don't ask what he shouldn't."

Miss Austen's face flushed fierily, and April used the opportunity to escape. She fled to the kitchen to order tea.

When Piers strolled into his aunt's ballroom, he was not surprised to see Sir Jeremy Gadsby acting as host for the occasion. He *was* surprised by how much his cousin Gussie's grin of pleasure touched him. Not that he was allowed much time to appreciate it, for before he even reached her, Aunt Hortensia, the Dowager Lady Petteril was glaring at him, and continued to do so as she gave him her hand in official welcome.

"How could you?" her ladyship demanded, her eyes cold and bitter.

He bowed over her hand. "You invited me. Or at least Bertie said you did."

"Don't speak to me of Bertie. We'll talk later."

Not if Piers could avoid it.

Gussie looked as if she might have hugged him but remembered her manners and her coiffure in time, and merely offered her hand and cheek for him to kiss, smiling widely the whole time.

"Cousin Piers! I'm so glad you are here for my ball, though I suppose you won't dance with me."

"You wouldn't like it if I did," he assured her. He looked her up and down. "You're looking much too lovely and will have far too much fun. Enjoy it."

Gussie was obliged to give her attention to the next arriving guest, and Gadsby, his cousin Maria's husband, gave him his hand.

"Evening, Petteril. Glad you could come." His voice lowered. "Don't mind her ladyship. She's furious about Bertie but it will pass."

They exchanged a look of understanding that was quite unexpected considering their last meeting when Piers had deliberately shamed Gadsby—and the rest of them—for stealing and sponging. In fact, Gadsby looked a great deal better than he had then—healthier and happier.

"Maria will be glad to see you," he assured Piers before he moved away. "We're living in the country now but couldn't miss Gussie's ball."

"Of course not," Piers murmured.

Leaving the only people who seemed familiar, he moved into the sea of strange faces, adopting his role of aloof viscount as he went, a faint, impersonal smile on his lips so that no acquaintance would be offended if he passed them by. There must have been a few, because some people caught his eye and bowed or smiled. With no idea who the devil they were, he inclined his head and kept moving.

For some reason, he had always had difficulty recognizing and distinguishing between faces that were not very familiar to him or were outside the context with which he associated them. Parties like this one were therefore something of a nightmare, a social disaster waiting to happen, and it was why he never danced. He had found that playing a role, like an actor on the stage, helped. In fact, it was all that had held him together when he first came to London as the viscount. Now it seemed to be part of him.

Accepting a sparkling glass from a passing footman, he strolled around the room until he felt more comfortable, and Sir Peter Haggard intercepted him.

"The Austens are here," Haggs murmured.

"I trust no one is shunning them?"

"Not noticeably. It seems no one is aware that Austen is genuinely suspected. The Bootles' accusations just seem like lashing out in grief. No one is taking them seriously. The scandal of him dying in Mrs. Eastleigh's house is delicious enough."

"It helps that the Bootles are in mourning and don't go out much," Piers said wryly.

"For now. But it would probably help if you spent some time with the Austens. I have the first dance with Miss Louise."

"It would help more if we found out who was truly responsible for Barret Bootle's death."

"No useful discoveries as yet, I gather?"

"Sadly, no. Not since a very promising villain turned out to have an alibi. But to implicate Percy smacks of enmity, to him as well as to Bootle."

"Likable fellow, Austen," Haggs said. "If he has that kind of enemy, I don't know who it can be. More to the point, neither does he."

There was little time for more, since the orchestra was introducing the first dance. Louise Austen, looking pretty in a pale green gown with exquisite embroidery across the hem and bosom, flushed a little as she gave her hand first to Piers in greeting, and then to Haggard for the dance.

Piers stayed talking to Percy for a little. Although a crowded ballroom was hardly the place to discuss murder, he did manage to ask Percy if he had ever met anyone from Mrs. Eastleigh's past.

"Either when you were together, or more recently," Piers murmured.

Percy shook his head. "She cut all ties with her past when she came to me. She never told me much, and to be honest, I didn't want to know. I didn't want to think about the hardship or the squalor of her life before."

"Then she never went back to visit her old friends?"

"No. She talked about it once or twice in the beginning. There was some child she was concerned about, and a couple of friends her own age, but I didn't want her going back there, let alone bringing anyone less savoury into her new life."

"You forbade her?" Piers asked, seeing a surprising new side to his old friend.

Percy flushed, shifting his stance and casting a quick glance around to be sure he was not overheard. "Not exactly. I just...discouraged her. She wanted to be a lady, with my help, so she had to leave all the old life behind her." He lowered his voice further. "I doubt Bootle would have let her, either. Though by then I doubt she wanted to."

Piers nudged him. "Forget about it for tonight. Go and dance."

Austen smiled and strolled toward a young lady and her chaperone. Piers moved about the room, mostly listening, though also responding to anyone who engaged him in conversation. He had very little idea who most of these people were, though some he could guess from what they said.

A few people spoke in hushed voices about the Bootle murder, but since it was hardly a fit topic for a ball, the subject quickly died. Mrs. Eastleigh's name was mentioned in hushed tones by some, but Percy Austen's was not. Yet.

Piers's mind was too wrapped up in the issue for him to spot Aunt Hortensia in time to avoid her.

"What are you about now?" her ladyship demanded, skewering him with her gaze. Her voice was low, though her eyes spat with all the old anger and resentment. "Are you trying to kill off the entire family?"

Piers blinked. "No, Aunt, and I can't imagine why such a thought should enter your head."

"Don't pretend to be a bigger imbecile than you can help. You have sent Bertie to die on the Peninsula. Just like John."

"I never sent John anywhere in my life," he said—mildly, since he had a certain sympathy for her. He even shared it. "As for Bertie, I merely gave him the money for promotion."

She curled her lip. "*Now*, you turn generous? To shuffle him out of the country and get killed by foreign heathens?"

"I don't think you can call them heathens," he said reasonably. Since this hardly calmed her fury, he added hastily, "Lots of officers go to Spain and don't die. And if you ask me—which, of course, I know you won't—it will do Bertie the world of good."

"Don't dress it up, Piers. You made it perfectly plain in March that you want us all gone!"

Piers ran out of patience. The imperious viscount raised one eyebrow. "I believe I requested you all to stop stealing from me. I voiced no interest at all in where you do it and indeed, I have none." He bowed slightly as her jaw dropped, then strolled off toward the mist of green that denoted Louise Austen.

He found Louise's company soothing after his aunt's entirely unfair attack. Bertie, he noticed, was smiling a good deal and looking rather pleased with himself.

"Thanks, Piers," he said in passing. "The matter is concluded, and I sail at the end of the week."

"Good luck," Piers said genuinely.

Bertie hesitated. "Aunt Hortensia is furious with us both."

"It has more to do with John than with you or me. Don't get killed and she'll come around."

Bertie uttered a shout of laughter and Piers and Miss Austen strolled on.

"Families," Louise observed.

"Families," he agreed. A sudden thought struck him. "I don't suppose there is anyone in yours who either dislikes Percy enough to implicate him in murder, or is protective enough to—er... do in his rivals in love?"

Louise closed her mouth which had begun to gape. "One has the oddest conversations with you, my lord."

"True, but that is not an answer."

She looked at him. "Do you really need one? Can you imagine my aunt shooting strangers with my brother's duelling pistol? Other than by accident, of course. Or are you accusing me?"

"Of course I was not. I know you and your aunt were at a ball on the night of the murder. I don't suppose you saw Lord Dilworth or Mrs. Bootle there, too?"

A breath of laughter escaped her. "No, actually, I did not."

"Never mind. April can probably find out from the servants."

"Is that why you employ her?" She was not looking at him now. In fact, her expression said she wished she had not asked.

Piers said, "One of the reasons." He would not talk about April, but Miss Austen looked so mortified that he set out to entertain her instead and succeeded so well that the lady was still laughing when a bluff young man came to claim her for the next dance.

Chapter Six

Since Barret's murder, Anne Eastleigh did not sleep well. She rose early and, leaving Jenny to cook the rest of the breakfast and make tea, she stepped out to the baker's shop on the corner to buy some fresh bread rolls. They were still warm and smelled delicious.

It was as she returned that a slow-moving carriage halted beside her, and Captain Jace stuck his head out of the window.

"Hello, Annie, love. I thought you were going to walk right past me."

She would have liked to. Instead, she stopped, casting a quick, furtive glance around her. "Not here, Jace."

"What? Too la-di-dah to talk to old friends in the street, now?"

"Certain old friends might reduce my income," she said sharply.

"You can't mean me, Annie," Jace mocked.

"What you want?" she asked.

"Just looking after you, like I always did. And reminding you..." He smiled, showing a gold tooth and a black one. "Payment due on Tuesday."

Dear God, how was she going to pay him off with no money coming in? She wished she had walked away, but in fact, the carriage took off before she did, and in a cloud of dust that left her coughing.

Fortunately, Annie was optimistic by nature and didn't let the encounter with Jace spoil the beauty of the morning or her enjoyment of breakfast. After breakfast, however, she had an unexpected visitor.

According to Stewart, his lordship's taciturn valet, Lord Petteril had been up early as usual to go out riding, despite his late night at the ball, and meant to give his usual reading lesson at nine. But when April breezed into the library a few minutes early, she found him asleep in his favourite chair at the fireside.

She paused, wondering whether or not to wake him before the others arrived. He had changed out of his riding dress into the smart buff pantaloons and well-fitting blue coat that were considered fashionable morning dress. Both quizzing glasses hung around his neck, and his cravat was tidily tied. Only his hair looked somewhat rumpled, but that seemed so much part of who he was that its lack of a combing made her smile.

In sleep, his face was unusually still, and she realized afresh how handsome he was with his sharp cheekbones, long, aristocratic nose and high, clever forehead. He had a well-shaped, mobile mouth that betrayed his true vulnerability while he slept.

She felt guilty for looking when he didn't know, and yet it was hard to turn away. His long legs stretched out in front of the fire. Something tingled in the pit of her stomach and her throat felt suddenly dry. What was the matter with her?

Annoyed with herself, she turned away and began crashing around with books and slates and writing materials on the larger table.

"Am I in disgrace?" he asked mildly.

She swung on him, scowling with suspicion. "What d'you mean?"

"You sound angry."

"Not with you," she said. "How was the ball?"

"Pleasant in parts. Excruciating in others." He stretched, and she looked hastily away, adjusting a chair that was already perfectly positioned. "But if you mean did I learn anything useful, then no. If there is gossip about Percy's involvement in Bootle's death, it is still very quiet."

She nodded. "Were the Austens there? At the ball?"

"Yes. Pity the Bootles could not be. It is a useful way to observe people without them noticing."

"You think one of them croaked Barret?"

"There is an unpleasant atmosphere in that house."

"And among the servants," April said. "But no one's talking. Not about anything that matters. Want me to see if I can catch someone else on their day off?"

"Might as well. We have nothing else."

"What will you do?"

Lord Petteril considered. "I might go and see your Annie."

"Why?" she asked at once.

He met her gaze. "Because I have no past with her. I might see her more clearly."

"She didn't do it."

"No, I don't suppose she did," Petteril said peaceably, as his other students came into the room.

"Lord Dilworth, ma'am," Jenny said with considerable awe.

Surprise pinned Annie to her chair until the man actually walked into her parlour, when she finally rose and curtsied. It was not the first time he had been here, but it was the first time without Barret and others being present. She couldn't recall him ever addressing a word directly to her.

A year or two older than Barret, he was also taller and leaner. His features might have been more regular, but the faint arrogance always present in Barret's expression looked like sheer temper in his brother's.

"How can I help your lordship?" Annie asked in her best ladylike accent—which was really rather good.

"By paying your rent on time, obviously, and agreeing not to use the house to gain immoral earnings."

With difficulty, she prevented her jaw from dropping. "I do not pay rent and you are insulting."

"You do now if you expect to live here. I inherit all Barret's worldly goods. I acknowledge he wished you to carry on living here if you so desire, but you will pay me rent or be evicted. My solicitor will be in touch. As for insults, we need not discuss it." He smiled. "You are, after all, in my house."

Annie's world reeled all over again. Somehow, she remained upright and perfectly still, when what she wanted to do was fly at him and smack him full in his smug, smirking face.

"Your solicitor may contact mine. Good day, my lord," she said.

At least it wiped the smile off his face for the briefest moment, before he said, "You need not offer payment in kind, Mrs. Eastleigh.

I was never one for soiled goods. Good day." He didn't march out. He strolled, as though the house really were his own.

Annie waited until the front door shut before she sank back down in her chair and wondered where the devil she was supposed to find rent without a protector? She would have to go out again, among her actress friends and attract someone suitable. She did not doubt her ability, only she was not ready. Her heart remembered Barret. Something in her had changed since the squalid days of St. Giles and Haymarket.

She didn't know how long she sat there before Jenny reappeared. "Ma'am? *He*'s here again."

Annie's head snapped up in time to see Captain Jace barge past Jenny without gentleness.

Annie had had enough. "What's the matter with you?" she said angrily, with all the aggression of her old accent. "Moved your entire business west, have you? Or just dodging the law?"

Jace looked amused, helping himself to a comfortable seat on the sofa. "Can't imagine why you'd think so."

"In Kensington at eight in the morning? Still here at almost midday? And you said you wanted paid on Tuesday. It's only Saturday."

"I said *by* Tuesday. Nah, I saw that nob come out your house and thought I'd call in to make sure you was well."

"I'll be better when you sling your hook."

He tutted. "Now then, Annie, your origins is showing. What'd the nob want?"

"He's my Barret's brother," she snapped. "Came to see how I was doing, of course. Jace, I don't want you round here. You'll queer my pitch."

Jace grinned and she suddenly realized that was what he wanted. That's why he made her pay for his silence, so she'd go short and have to go back to work for him. In sudden panic, she jerked her gaze free. Dear God, how was she to pay off Jace *and* Dilworth? She'd have to flee London altogether, only that went against the grain.

"Bugger off, Jace," she snarled, just as Jenny opened the door again.

"Ma'am, that lord's here again."

"Dilworth?" Annie said, appalled.

"The other one."

Jace stared at her. "You interviewing for the position?" he demanded.

"Bugger off," she repeated between her teeth.

Jace laughed and rose, but by then Lord Petteril was walking into the room, looking gentlemanly and fashionable with his quizzing glasses and elegant, gold-topped cane. He obviously clocked Jace at once, but it was to Annie he bowed.

"Good afternoon, Mrs. Eastleigh, might I beg a moment of your time?"

She curtsied and threw Jace a significant look, which meant, *See, that's how a gentleman behaves.* Not that Jace would understand either the look or the gentleman.

"Don't worry, I'm on my way out." Jace leered. "I'll leave the two of you alone together. Goodbye my sweet!" He strolled past Lord Petteril, who didn't move apart from a faint twitch of the nostrils, and began whistling in the passage.

"He's gone!" Jenny shouted from the front door, and Annie let herself sag back into her chair. She'd been doing a lot of that today.

"Who's he?" Petteril asked, strolling to the window and raising his quizzing glass to peer out at the coach.

"Mr. Marr?" Annie said breezily. "No one."

Lord Petteril turned. "*Jason* Marr? Was that the notorious Captain Jace?"

Annie felt the blood drain from her face. "How do you know him?"

"Oh, I don't. April mentioned his name."

"Well, I won't say he is welcome in my house," Annie said grandly. "But as an acquaintance from my past—which I'm sure you know all about—I speak to him now and again."

"Did he know Mr. Bootle, too?" Lord Petteril asked.

Annie shuddered. "God, no." Her breath caught suddenly. "You're never thinking *Jace* killed Barret?"

"It crossed my mind," his lordship said. "But he has an alibi."

"A what?"

"He was somewhere else. He couldn't have done it."

"Just as well. Don't fancy the law's chances of catching him, let alone hanging him. Which is a pity in some ways. What can I do for you, my lord?"

"If you wouldn't mind showing me where you kept the pistol."

"I don't mind," she said, rising once more, "though I don't know what good it'll do."

He only smiled. He had a nice smile, April's lord. In fact, there was something very appealing about him. He was like quicksilver, moving and changing shape, from the arrogant fribble of an aristo he had shown to Jace, to the amiable, almost boyish cove who followed her eagerly into the study. April said he was bookish, too. And kind, though Annie reserved judgement on that. She'd known other men who looked kind.

She went over to the desk and opened the drawer. There was no lock. And there was the empty space where the pistol had lain, next to a small box of powder and four balls lying loose.

"Percy wanted me to keep it in the bedchamber at night," she recalled. "But I never did. I wouldn't even let him load it. Shoved it in there out the way. I don't like guns."

"Noisy things," he agreed. "Who else knew it was here?"

"Just Barret and me. And Jenny."

He glanced up at the door, frowning. "So, someone managed to come in through the front door, walk in here, reach past Bootle for the gun, load it... Sorry," he added as she shuddered. "Thinking aloud. But it doesn't make much sense, does it?"

"Not unless he'd fallen asleep," she said, "though even then, the murderer would have had to know it was there. Bit too lucky to walk into an occupied room and just find it."

"That's what I thought. Although Barret might have had it out and loaded it himself for whatever reason. Perhaps he was expecting someone."

"I don't know who, and he never said he was. He said he'd have a quick brandy and come to bed."

Lord Petteril's long, elegant fingers passed over the pistol balls, lifting one distractedly. Then he stilled. "Four balls. How many balls did Percy give you?"

"Just the four. Like I say, I never meant to use any of them."

"Yet we are meant to believe that someone did. And there are four balls still here."

Plus one in Barret's head. Annie rubbed her forehead, perplexed. "What does that mean? That Percy's pistol didn't kill Barret after all?"

Lord Petteril smiled dazzlingly, which rather caught at the breath. "Exactly. Someone killed him with another weapon entirely and dropped Percy's pistol on the floor beside him, solely to implicate you. Or Percy."

Annie began to smile. "Then Percy's in the clear! That's worth a cup of tea! And then you'd better run and tell poor Percy!"

Mrs. Eastleigh was so genuinely delighted by this discovery in Austen's favour that Piers did not have the heart to tell her that it didn't entirely exonerate him. Austen could, in theory, have brought another loaded pistol with him. Or more ammunition. But since the case against him rested largely on the fact that the murder weapon was his, things really looked much better.

"If we'd both just told the truth in the beginning, he'd never have had that cloud of suspicion hanging over him," Annie said ruefully. "Or me!"

They were having a celebratory cup of tea in the parlour, and Annie, looking as if a huge weight had been lifted from her shoulders, was positively sparkling. Piers began to see the attraction that had captivated both Austen and Barret. And the basic kindness behind the fun that had earned April's devotion.

"They were understandable lies, and we can correct them easily enough." Piers sipped his tea from a rather fine porcelain cup and set it on the saucer. "But we still need to know who *did* shoot Barret. Someone who hated both him and Percy and knew where the pistol was kept."

"Well it wasn't Jenny and it wasn't me," Annie said tartly. "And it sure as hell wasn't Barret."

He regarded her thoughtfully. "You and Jenny and Barret are the only people you are *aware* of who knew about the pistol. Who else has been in the house? Didn't your friends visit you here?"

"A few. Theatre people mostly."

"Did they always stay in one room?"

She opened her mouth, then closed it again. "No. Not of an evening. And often they were here when Barret brought friends, too."

"Any of your theatre friends have cause to dislike Barret?"

"No, he was hospitable and tolerant, and if you're thinking he bothered the girls and caused ill-feeling, he didn't and he wouldn't."

Piers let that pass. Barret was already unfaithful to his wife, although he did appear to have been devoted to Annie. "Did any of these people know Percy, too?"

"Only Barret and his friends, I think. After me, Percy pretty much avoided the Haymarket ware."

"Who were the friends Barret brought?"

"Frequently?" She counted them off on her fingers. "George Horton. Captain Withan. Tommy Keyes. Toby—Lord Dilworth—came a couple of times, too. There were others, but only once, I think. I can't see any of them shooting Barret like that." She sniffed. "Except Dilworth."

"How often did Captain Withan visit?" Though Piers had difficulty believing his cousin capable of such a crime, it crossed his mind uneasily that it could well be the reason for Bertie's sudden desire to serve abroad.

"Two or three times. Amusing fellow with a roving eye. I quite liked him. Is he a friend of yours?"

"We're acquainted." And Bertie had no reason, so far as he was aware, to hate Percy Austen. He doubted they even knew each other. Bertie had denied it, though Piers intended to find out for certain, and discover what he could about the others Annie had mentioned. He switched subjects with deliberate abruptness. "What is it you are not telling me about Jason Marr?"

That wiped the smile off her face so quickly that he felt guilty. "It's nothing to do with the murder," she said. "You told me he was somewhere else and couldn't have done it."

"Nevertheless, I would like to help if I can. April would never forgive me if I did not."

Her eyes softened for an instant, and then a look of weary, tolerant scorn filled them. "With all respect, sir, the likes of you don't deal with the likes of him. He don't play by your rules. Or any rules at all. Even the hardest, the toughest and the wiliest, step carefully around Captain Jace. I thought I'd got away from him when I came here with Percy. But he found me. I paid him to stay away. You saw him. I can't be respectable with the likes of him hanging around. I even told him Barret knew about him and wouldn't let me pay him anymore. Complete lie, of course. Never told Barret nothing about Jace, and Jace just said it was up to me to find the money from somewhere. Bastard. And don't tell me my accent's slipped again, because I know it. He brings out the worst in me."

"He has not stayed away," Piers observed.

"No, well, he's worried I can't pay him now Barret is not providing for me." A bleakness washed over her and she shrugged. "I'll have to think of something because I'm not going back to him or to St. Giles."

"Did Barret not leave you provided for?"

"Left the house to his brother with his wish that I live in it as long as I want to. But Dilworth wants to charge me rent."

"That seems very...cheeseparing."

She wrinkled her nose. "No wonder Barret didn't like him."

"Actually, I was referring to Barret. Did he leave a will?"

"Yes, but—"

"If you don't have a solicitor, I'll have mine look into it for you. It does seem unnecessarily mean."

She closed her mouth on whatever she had been going to say, and merely gazed at him, "Thank you," she said at last, then almost immediately, "What are you doing with my Ape?"

He raised one eyebrow. "Employing her."

"You made her back into a girl."

"She was an increasingly less convincing boy. She only got away with it at all because she was half-starved. I couldn't let her sleep with the grooms." He gazed intensely into his teacup as though it could provide him with courage. He had to force out the words. "How bad was it for her?"

"About as bad as it can be," Annie said steadily, and he had to close his eyes to hide the pain, though he couldn't prevent the frown. "I wasn't there and I don't know the detail. But I know the signs, the look in the eyes. And something made her leave the river and the docks. She slept in doorways round St. Giles, grabbing bits of food like a stray dog. Wouldn't let anyone touch her. Fought like a cat or ran for it. Feral she were. *He* were. We all thought he was a lad then, gave him the odd meal, slipped him a penny for running errands, till at least he realized not *everyone* would hurt him. I only discovered he were a girl by accident. You going to have the vapours if I mention female complaints?"

He opened his eyes. "No."

"Well, she had hers before she could hide it from me. We covered it up between us and I never told anyone. We helped each other out after that, when we could. We were friends. I worried about him when I left. In fact, I wanted him to come with me but he wouldn't." Her eyes, which had lost focus as she remembered the past, fixed once more on his face. "This life, my life, isn't for her."

"I know that."

"Do you?" Annie said with a hint of derision. "Ape makes a beautiful girl, even in that daft cap you have her wearing. And you're aware of it. A woman like me spots these things."

He found it increasingly hard to be still, but he had asked for her honesty and perhaps she deserved his. Up to a point.

"She is my friend."

Annie stared at him. "She's your servant."

But he had found the only truth that mattered and held her gaze without difficulty now. "She is my friend."

Chapter Seven

"It's the brother," April said with excitement when Piers had told her about his visit to Annie. "He certainly sounds horrible enough to croak his own kin and to put the blame on someone else."

"Maybe," Piers said, pacing between the library door and the window. "But why now? The brothers lived in the same house, happily quarrelling, for years. Why kill him last Monday? And why leave Austen's pistol at the scene to implicate him?"

"He was probably trying to implicate Annie."

Piers shook his head. "No, it was Dilworth who recognized the pistol as Austen's. He saw Percy shooting with it at Manton's Gallery."

"True." She perched on the edge of the table, frowning. "But it still could have been him. Barret would have let his brother into the house at midnight, where he wouldn't have opened the door to anyone else. We know he'd been to the house before. He might well have known about the pistol in the study drawer. Which would explain how he placed the gun and still got out of the house so quick, before Annie and Jenny came rushing downstairs when the gun went off."

Piers paused by the window and nodded slowly. "That is true. And yet it takes a particular vindictiveness to implicate someone else for his own crime."

"Not *someone* else," April said cynically. "*Anyone* else."

"Maybe." He sighed. "But why now? Why kill his brother now when they'd disliked each other for years? There had to have been some worse quarrel than usual."

"Over Mrs. Bootle?" April said, straightening. Her breath caught. "Or Annie herself! Perhaps Dilworth wanted her!"

"And then threatens to evict her as soon as his brother is dead, if she doesn't start paying him rent?"

She slumped again. "Fair point. And he can't marry his brother's widow, can he?"

"No," he said in surprise. "At least not under ecclesiastical law. How do you know that?"

"Must have read it somewhere," she said vaguely, not really listening. Then, realizing what she had said, she glanced up and grinned at him. "I learn all sorts now."

He couldn't help smiling back, though it came with an odd pain. "You do and you will."

"What you have to do is cultivate the brother," April decided. "I can only learn so much from servants and they ain't really the talkative types. The family's having a memorial for him, followed by a breakfast, day after tomorrow. You should go, talk to this Dilworth."

"And the widow," he said thoughtfully. "She might not have known about the pistol, but I'm sure she knew about Annie. And if *she* had turned up at the door that night, Barret would have *had* to let her in. What I need, sadly, is more society gossip. Perhaps I shall call upon my cousins again—after I've seen Mr. Pepper."

She sprang up off the table. "Want me to come with you to the solicitor?"

He did. He liked her company and her insight. But Annie's revelations, however vague, were too recent. "No, I think you should spend as much time with Annie as you can. I'm sure there is more she's not telling us yet." He was already striding for the door and didn't look at her.

Only when he stepped into his curricle and took the reins did he recall that Jason Marr liked to call in on Annie. And he did not want that scum anywhere near April.

"Something wrong, my lord?" Benson asked.

Piers blinked at him. "No. No, I don't think so. Let 'em go!" Marr was not likely to turn up at Annie's house again today. And he would find something else for April to do tomorrow.

Cousin Maria and her husband, Sir Jeremy Gadsby, had given up their town house and were staying with Aunt Hortensia. Piers had been hard on them over the necklace affair, but any guilt he might have felt about what they had given up to pay their debt more quickly, vanished in the contentment that now radiated from them. Maria seemed to glow and confided to Piers that she was *enceinte* but had not yet told her mother. She had been packing to return to the country, now that Gussie's ball was passed.

"I had forgotten how much I like life in the country," she told Piers with a smile as she sat down in the pleasant back sitting room. "As if leaving Haybury Court meant I could no longer have a country home at all. But Barnett Hall is really rather lovely. We have charming neighbours and there is so much to do in the village."

"I'm glad to see you so happy."

She coloured slightly. "The necklace business was miserable. Jeremy says you gave us a much-needed kick, and he is right. We both thought the other preferred town life. And neither of us does! Is everything well with you, Piers?"

"Oh yes, of course. I wanted to ask you about Barbara Bootle. Is she a friend of yours?"

"I'm acquainted with her, of course, but we were never friends." A fleeting smile dawned. "No doubt I was a little fast for her, and I certainly found her somewhat dull."

"Was there no gossip about her?"

"Only that her husband found her dull, too. He rather raked around."

"Then Mrs. Eastleigh was not his only ladybird?"

Maria looked amused. "I don't believe you should speak to me of ladybirds. I don't know whom he favoured. Jeremy might."

"What of Lord Dilworth, his brother?"

"More social graces. Caused less gossip. I don't really know him either."

Gadsby, wandering in only a few minutes later, had a better acquaintance with Barret Bootle. Like Bertie, he even knew Mrs. Eastleigh, had been to her house to play cards one night and no doubt to ogle the actresses who were her not infrequent guests.

"Was he faithful to Mrs. Eastleigh?" Piers asked. "Or did he have other amours?"

"Faithful to Mrs. Eastleigh!" Maria exclaimed. "What about his poor wife?"

"I don't think he considered his wife at all," Gadsby said ruefully. "But he seemed to have given up chasing other women. It was almost as if he was married to Mrs. Eastleigh. And liked it."

"Who is Mrs. Eastleigh?" Gussie asked, almost bouncing into the room and grinning at Piers as she threw herself into the chair next to his.

"No one you will ever meet," Gadsby said austerely.

"Then why are you discussing her?" Aunt Hortensia demanded, having apparently followed her youngest offspring with rather more grace. "Is Piers considering marriage?"

"Good God, no," Piers said, startled. He had risen to bow and stood regarding her with some suspicion.

"Well, you should be," his aunt retorted. "Bertie is your only heir and you've sent him off to the Peninsula to be killed."

"Mama!" her daughters objected at once, which seemed to surprise her.

"What? He *does* need to marry, and sooner rather than later. We already know to our cost how quickly things can change."

It was as if she took satisfaction in lowering their spirits. Perhaps she did. She had lost her husband and two sons within a year. Piers tried to remember that and pity her. Mostly, he just disliked her.

"How well are you acquainted with the Bootles, Aunt?" he asked.

"I know Lady Kinsley, of course. And Kinsley offered for me once. I'm glad to say I turned him down. Bad blood in the Bootles. Just look at what happened to Barret."

"That was hardly his fault, Mama," Maria murmured.

"It is if he died in such a place!"

"It was Kensington, not Seven Dials," Gadsby pointed out. "Very respectable place, Kensington."

"Not if one is murdered there," Aunt Hortensia said with the air of one who has just incontrovertibly won the argument.

"What do you think of the family?" Piers asked, in a last gasp attempt to learn anything. "Are any of them bad-tempered, badly behaved, scandalous? What of Barbara Bootle?"

"I know nothing against any of them," Aunt Hortensia said regally.

"Except that there is bad blood in them," Gussie pointed out and received a glare.

“I believe Barret was a bit of a rake, quarrelled with his father and brother. And his wife.”

“He quarrelled openly with his wife?” Piers said quickly.

“At least once,” Aunt Hortensia said with relish. “I heard him. Dilworth took her part.”

“Did he?” Piers murmured. Chivalry? Or was there more to it? Was Barbara the cause of a new, more violent enmity between the brothers? Could Dilworth and Barret’s wife be lovers?

Difficult, under the nose of the parents...

“Why did Barret not move out of the parental home when he was married?” he asked.

“No money,” Gadsby said.

“He had money to set Mrs. Eastleigh up in her own house.” Piers pointed out.

“Piers!” warned his aunt.

“Can’t take a house in Mayfair for the price of one in Kensington,” Gadsby pointed out. “And I don’t see Barbara Bootle living in Kensington.”

“Dear me, no!” said Aunt Hortensia, clearly outraged by the very idea. She shuddered. “People are murdered there!”

Piers avoided his cousins’ eyes, though beside him, Gussie made an unladylike gurgling noise. “Do you know a Tommy Keyes? Or a George Horton?”

“You met Mr. Horton at Augusta’s ball,” Aunt Hortensia said witheringly. “He spoke to you for some time?”

“About carriages,” Gadsby said helpfully.

“Ah.” Piers recalled the conversation, which had been more amusing than informative, though he could remember nothing whatsoever of the man’s face. “Seemed a decent fellow.”

“Respectable family,” Hortensia pronounced. “Expectations from his childless uncle, Sir Francis.”

“No sense of responsibility,” Maria added, “but no malice either. He likes Gussie.”

“Gussie likes him,” Gussie said. “But she certainly won’t marry him. What was the other name?”

“Keyes,” Piers said.

“Widower,” said Hortensia, refocusing on Piers. “He married ridiculously young and has a daughter. She was at the ball, too. You could do worse.”

"I could," Piers agreed peaceably. "Is he a pleasant chap?"

"I always liked him," Gadsby said. "Went on a bit of a spree a few years ago when his wife died but has turned into a respectable Papa. Mostly."

Maria leaned forward. "What's your interest in all these people, Piers?"

"Oh, just trying to keep up," he said vaguely.

He departed shortly after, wishing Maria and Jeremy a safe journey home.

Although nothing solid or definite had come out of his gossip with his family, Piers had found a tangle of possible motives. Barret had been "wasting" money he could ill afford on a woman who was not his wife. He was slighting his wife and thereby angering his brother as well as Barbara. And if there was some kind of illicit relationship between Barbara and Barret's brother, the murder could even be a conspiracy. They had been together, or said they were, when Barret was murdered.

Riding in Hyde Park the following morning, Piers tried to think of a viable reason to call upon the family again. He hadn't managed to come up with much when, to his astonishment, he saw Lord Dilworth himself. Astride a decent black gelding and wearing a black cravat, he rode between Percy and Louise Austen.

Toby Bootle, who, as the heir to his father's earldom, bore the courtesy title Baron Dilworth, had been finding that even in death his brother succeeded in spoiling his own life. Now that the fool was dead, Dilworth had to deal with the misery of the family and the annoyance of Barret's mistress. To say nothing of the frustration of having to eschew parties and any other amusements, at least until the end of the month, when the best of the Season would be fizzling out.

An early ride was one of the few things he could still do without upsetting his parents, and for once luck was with him. Louise Austen was riding in the park, too. Admittedly she was with her brother, whom his father had more or less accused of murdering Barret after Dilworth had identified the pistol.

They both looked slightly stunned when he reined in his horse and doffed his hat. "Good morning, Miss Austen. Mr. Austen. A beautiful day, is it not?"

Austen moved instinctively closer to his sister and did not reply. Miss Austen however, said politely. "Indeed it is. I hope you will accept our condolences on the loss of your brother."

"Thank you, you are very kind." He could not leave it there. Not after sounding so excessively cheerful, and with Austen so white-lipped and stiff. "Actually, I'm glad I ran into you both. We need to clear the air, Austen."

"I did not shoot your brother or harm him in any way," Austen said flatly.

"I know that," Dilworth said at once. "I had to tell them the pistol was yours—you know yourself it is most distinctive—but truly it was not meant as an accusation. My father, prostrate with grief, would not be reasoned with. I told him it was more likely Mrs. Eastleigh herself or one of her low acquaintances. You have not been charged, have you, Austen?"

"Not yet," Austen said thinly.

"It should not happen now at all," Miss Austen added. "Mrs. Eastleigh admitted that Percy gave her the pistol years ago, along with the ammunition, all of which is still in place. It now looks as if that pistol was not the weapon that actually killed your brother and there is no reason to suspect Percy."

"Only whoever tried to implicate me," Austen said.

"Good Lord," Dilworth said, frowning and then letting his brow clear into a smile. He even stretched out his hand to Austen. "I am very glad to hear it. I hope you will forgive any part I played in this...unpleasantness."

Austen might have hesitated, but he was basically a good-natured man, and soon reached out to clasp Dilworth's hand while Louise smiled upon them both.

"May I join you for a little?" Dilworth asked.

They could hardly refuse. Even so, Dilworth was well on his way to returning to their good graces by the time another horseman joined them.

"Withy!" Austen greeted this fellow, whom Dilworth recognized as Lord Petteril upon a large, chestnut horse.

Petteril was an intriguing figure, whom he had found an odd acquaintance for Barret when he had called with his condolences. He was an academic, apparently, certainly eccentric and somewhat mercurial. Dilworth would have sought him out, since fashionable society seemed to find him so appealing. However, glancing at Miss Austen, he was hit by the unwelcome suspicion that Petteril intrigued her, too. There was a faint, pretty blush on her cheeks and a sparkle in her eyes as she wished him good morning.

"Do you know each other?" Austen asked.

"We have met," Dilworth said, offering his hand.

"How are you?" Petteril asked, leaning forward to clasp it. His eyes were direct and serious, as though he truly cared. Which was excessively kind when Dilworth would not miss his brother at all.

"Oh, coming to terms with things," Dilworth said vaguely.

"Grief takes time," Miss Austen assured him with a smile of sympathy that he was not above milking.

Petteril joined the group and they rode together toward the Cumberland gate, where Petteril left them. Although Louise Austen's eyes strayed after him, Dilworth was not disheartened. On the marriage mart, an eccentric viscount might have been desirable, but Dilworth would be an earl one day, and that easily trumped Viscount Petteril. Besides, whatever Austen thought, the aunt, Mrs. Manners, definitely favoured Dilworth.

April and Annie giggled over tea, addressing each other only in the refined accents of ladies. Annie had been teaching April, with often hilarious results.

"My dear, you are a natural," Annie told her, primly picking up her teacup.

"Why, thank you, Mrs. Eastleigh. I have been observing the nobs for some weeks now—"

"Miss Withan, you cannot call them—us!—*nobs*! We are ladies of quality."

"Then I have been observing his lordship and several of his acquaintances. I too can speak as if I had a mouthful of pebbles."

Annie snorted, inhaling her tea and hastily set down the cup while she coughed and spluttered.

"Mrs. Eastleigh, you have spilled your tea. Shall I send for the crow?"

"Physician, my dear Miss Withan."

"Withan is not my name," April announced.

"Who cares?" Annie replied. "I am not Mrs. Eastleigh either."

April laughed and reverted to normal speech. "Is Eastleigh not even your real name?"

"Yes, that's real enough. But you know as well as I do I've never been married."

"Well, don't call me Withan, eh? Himself wouldn't like it."

"I don't know. You wouldn't be the first servant to take their master's name. You got one of your own? If you have, I never heard it."

April frowned, then shrugged. "Don't remember. I never needed it. I was just Ape and now I'm April."

"Respectable people have surnames. You should pick one."

Returning to refined accents, they spent another few minutes coming up with increasingly silly surnames. At "Miss Gogglesworth-Silly," April fell off her chair laughing and needed some gasping time to recover.

Then, for a few moments, she lay on the floor, gazing at the ceiling. "You like this house, Annie?"

"I do. Imagine Barret's own brother lying about it, pretending it was his when Barret left it to me!"

"I think they're short of money," April said, sitting up.

Annie stared at her. "And Dilworth killed his brother to lower their expenses?"

April bent her knees, sliding her feet back and forth across the carpet. "Maybe. His lordship's going to the memorial service tomorrow, and back to the house. I'm going to be serving the breakfast."

Annie looked stricken. "How did you manage that, then?"

It seemed even sadder, because she kept her refined accent. April swallowed. "They're taking on extra staff for the event. Then I can poke around while everyone else is engaged. It's wrong you can't be there, Annie, when you loved him best."

"I did," Annie whispered.

"Surely they can't stop you going to the church?"

"I won't cause a scene. I'll remember Barret my own way."

April nodded and climbed slowly back into her chair to finish her tea. "Anyhow, at least we sorted out Lord Dilworth's game. Now, what are we going to do about Captain Jace?"

Annie sighed. "Keep paying him I suppose. Never knew anyone get the better of Jace, did you?"

April shook her head. "Don't mean it can't be done. Don't it seem odd to you that he's hanging around here so much? Ain't he got nothing to do in St. Giles no more?"

"He's just trying to frighten me. Doesn't know what I'll do next or how I'm fixed."

April blinked. "How much money you been giving him?"

"Not enough, obviously. He wants me to go back—thinks I'd be a great earner for him now I'm refined. Wish whoever shot Barret had shot that bastard instead."

"So do I." In fact, even if Jace had shot Barret it would be better. The law would finally hang him. "But wishes never did nothing."

Chapter Eight

That evening, in her pleasant little bedchamber in Petteril House, April struggled back into her boy's clothes. She hadn't worn them since the day in the country she'd found the highwayman Brandy Bill. Even then, she thought, staring with displeasure at her reflection in the glass, she must have been taking a bit of a chance.

Now, the clothes didn't fit her at all. She'd filled out too much at the chest and the hips. Too much decent food. She hadn't put on much weight, though, for she could still fasten the clothes. The trouble was the curves. She looked like a girl. Even with the old, baggy jacket, which covered the worst of it, she looked like a girl.

She couldn't be Ape anymore. There was a sense of loss in that knowledge, but not much. Certainly not as much as she had expected. Being Ape might have been simpler in her old haunts, but worst of all would be discovery anywhere near Jace as a girl dressed as a boy.

She took off Ape's clothes and shoved them to the back of the cupboard. Where Ape really belonged. He'd never been real anyway, just a means of getting her through the days and months and years...

She found the dress with the tear in it, and the cap that the kitchen maid had spilled gravy on at dinner yesterday. She hid all her growing blonde curls under the cap and fastened the dress unevenly, hiking it over her belt to look as if it was too short and too wide to fit. Ape's boots were actually useful to complete the picture, as was the rouge she'd borrowed from Annie. She used it to redden patches on her face and neck and hands. Now she looked as if she had some kind of skin complaint and been hit a few times into the bargain. She added a spot of kohl—also borrowed from Annie—to look like an incipient black eye. If nothing else, it contributed to the overall impression of grubbiness.

Finally, she pulled a thin shawl from the laundry heap and added that to her ensemble. She would do.

His lordship had invited Percy Austen and Sir Peter Haggard to dine, so the staff were all busy serving dinner. No one noticed her, head down, wandering into the scullery, sliding her hands over leftovers on the plate and wiping them on her clothes as she walked out and along the passage to the area door.

It had been almost depressingly easy to get out of the house unnoticed and unseen. Lord Petteril had been oddly distant over the last couple of days. He had discussed the murder and Annie and the Bootles with her, and even helped with her understanding of the book she was trying to read. But something was missing, and that hurt.

No one did aloof like the viscount, of course. But he wasn't quite that. She didn't feel his protection had been withdrawn, or even the connection that had bound them since she'd first burgled his house and found him trying to jump off the upstairs balcony. It just felt as if he was no longer acknowledging these things. That she was no longer special.

Well, she couldn't be, could she? She was a thief from the St. Giles gutters and he was a lord. The novelty was bound to wear off. Not the loyalty but the illusion of friendship. As he found his feet, he didn't need her. She was glad of that, even proud of that. But it hurt all the same.

Maybe it was for the best. The happiness she felt around him wasn't right. It wasn't right that she should watch him sleeping stretched out before the fire with his handsome face and his sensitive hands and long, elegant legs, and *feel...*

She hurried faster along the road, head well down, looking out for a hackney that would take her at least part of the way toward St. Giles.

She smelled it first. After the country, the whole of London smelled, but these streets stank of human effluence and rotting food, open sewers and unwashed bodies. She had almost forgotten the noise and the closeness of other people.

Dear God, no wonder Annie won't go back.

Neither would April, and she *would* help her friend. Her heart beating with memory and fear, she walked around a bit, trying to look as if she had a plan but in reality looking for her nerve again.

She had got too used to safety and comfort and she really, *really* didn't want to be here. But she owed Annie. That debt could never be paid, but she had to do whatever she could. She had to get Jace off her back, and to know how, she had to know what the hell Jace was up to.

She was circling closer to the Queen's Head, letting the familiarity of the place back in until she was part of it again. She began to recognize people: the blind beggar with the dog that shoved its head under her hand—it didn't care that she was wearing skirts now; the baker who'd chased her up the road with a club when she'd prigged a stale bread roll; a couple of prostitutes she'd run errands for. She had a nasty moment when a man brushed past her and she recognised Lord, the thief she'd used to work for and stupidly imagined was her key to get out of St. Giles.

Well, and so he was indirectly.

Her knees almost gave way, but Lord didn't even look at her.

Outside the Queen's Head, she approached a couple of women talking and sharing a flask of something. She didn't know them at all, so they must have been new.

One of them lowered the flask, her gaze hostile. "What you want, then?"

"Looking for work," April said, adding hastily before anyone hit her or worse. "Just sweeping the floors like. Odd jobs, serving food and drink. D'you know if there's anything going here?"

"Shouldn't think so." The woman looked her up and down with amiable contempt. "You ain't his type."

"Don't want to be anyone's type." April sniffed. "Just need to eat."

"Don't we all," said the other woman. "You could ask him, but he won't look at you for upstairs."

April had no intention of going upstairs—she had always avoided it like the plague, even when she'd swaggered in with Lord. "What's he like then? Don't suppose he'd pay up front if I asked? Just for one shift?"

"Him? Not a chance. Step over you if you was dying, he would. Probably kick you and all. You'd be better round the Silver Jug. Tatty likes someone to sweep up and guard the place over night. Means you got somewhere to kip and all."

"Tatty sent me here," April said morosely. "He seemed to think it was funny. Here, this captain ain't out of business, or taken up by the law, is he?"

"Not yet," said the first girl cynically. "Got competition, though, ain't he? Madam Ells round the corner got new girls and taking his business. And some of his popular whores. She pretends they're quality, fallen on hard times, but they ain't. No better 'n us. But she's smarter than him and he don't like it."

Her friend kicked her with casual brutality. "Shut your mouth, Nan. How much of that have you had? He'll black your eyes for talking like that."

"He sounds too scary for me," April mumbled, edging away. "Maybe I'll ask this Mrs. Ells..."

It was dark by the time she came home, and the only light in the house shone faintly through the window beside the area door. At least she wouldn't have to break in through the bars of the pantry window as she had the first time she'd come here. She wondered if she would still fit.

She crept down the area steps and tapped lightly on the door. She hoped it would be Mr. Park who would merely look down his nose and refer her to his wife, the housekeeper, for punishment. Then, by the time she was faced with Mrs. Park in the morning, she would have thought of some story to keep her sweet...

The door opened and she had whisked inside before she realized the candlelight shone not on Mr. Park in his shirt sleeves but on Lord Petteril.

Her stomach gave one sickening dive.

"Thanks," she said breezily. "You shouldn't be down here watching the doors, you know. See you in the—"

His hand closed over her shoulder as she would have slipped past him and bolted for the servants' stairs.

"No, I shouldn't," he agreed, staring down at her. "What happened to you?"

"Nothing. It's just Annie's rouge and a bit of kohl..."

A sound like a groan escaped him. Equally, it might have been a laugh, but his face didn't lighten and he didn't let her go. "Where have you been, April?"

She didn't struggle. If anyone else had touched her, she'd have been on the other side of the room by now. Or he would have been.

"Just looking into some things for Annie," she said carelessly. "I think Cap'n Jace wants her back to add more class to the Queen's Head. A new brothel opened up round the corner and it's eating into his profits. Reckon Lord and Tatty and the others will be making the most of his weakness."

Lord Petteril's anger was not like other people's. She had never heard him yell and he never lashed out, but his eyes turned hard and cold, with a glitter that would cut glass. His mouth tightened, with a faint upward twitch to the left corner that conveyed the utter contempt that she had prayed never to have it turned on her.

It was turned on her now.

She swallowed. The blood seemed to have drained from her lips, leaving them unmanageable. "I'm sorry. I wish you hadn't waited up. How'd you know I was gone?"

"Because no one could find you when I asked. Mrs. Park didn't know where you were. Or said she didn't."

"I didn't tell her."

His fingers gripped harder for an instant, then loosened and he snatched them away, but not before she realized they were shaking.

"*No one* knew where you were April," he said. "You went to St. Giles without telling a soul. How were we supposed to find you if something happened?"

Shame flooded her, but still she prevaricated, trying to work out his emotion because it wasn't anger after all, or at least not *only* anger. "How d'you know I went to St. Giles?"

"I can smell it."

She drew in her breath, gazing at his broad back and his tangled hair. "I didn't tell you because I didn't want to..." *I didn't want to worry you.* She closed her eyes and told the truth. "You wouldn't have let me go."

He swung on her, almost savage in the light flickering from his sudden movement. "And you know there is good reason for that!"

She should have stepped back, out of his reach, but she didn't. She was too busy searching his face, his eyes, a frown tugging at her own brow. She had worried him. But more than anxiety, she read something closer to terror. The sort of terror she always felt at the idea of him sending her away, of losing him in some other way, and God knew that only got worse.

"I was careful," she whispered. "I know how to look after myself, and I kept out of the way of anyone who could hurt me. I needed to know, for Annie."

Their eyes locked in some dreadful, dangerous intimacy. And yet something lightened within her because she saw that he could no more break the connection than she could. It made no real difference. She would never be more than the thief-servant-assistant and he would always be the viscount. And it didn't matter.

"I'll make you some hot chocolate," she said and tore free, throwing off her shawl and bustling about the kitchen, pouring milk into a pan for heating on the stove.

He was so silent she thought he had left in silent fury, or at least in the pretence of it. She didn't look, because she wanted to go on imagining he was there, just for a few minutes longer.

But when she turned with two big cups of steaming chocolate, he was sitting on a chair on the other side of the table, watching her. She set the cups down, pushed one toward him, and sank into the chair opposite his. With peculiar sweetness, it reminded her of the first night she had stayed here.

"How does this help Annie?" he asked at last.

"I don't know yet," she admitted. "But we'll think of something."

"I suppose we will."

She smiled into her cup, with perfect faith in their joint ingenuity.

"April?" he said.

"Yes?"

"I want your promise this time. You don't go there again, not for anything or anyone."

It was a price she was prepared to pay. "All right. I promise."

From the memorial service for Barret Bootle in St. George's Church, Hanover Square, it was a short walk to Kinsley House. Few people summoned their carriages. Piers walked with Haggard and Percy Austen, well behind Lord Kinsley and Lord Dilworth.

"No one's looking at me as if I did him in," Austen murmured.

"They will if they overhear remarks like that," Haggs replied. "Decent turn-out, don't you think?"

As the son of an earl, and a politically active one at that, it was probably inevitable. But many of the mourners were younger men, so many that Piers was almost daunted. If the murderer was not Dilworth or Mrs. Bootle, then the net of suspicion was cast wider. Since nothing, with the possible exception of a single cuff link, had been stolen from Annie's house, it was unlikely to be a passing thief. The killer had to have had a reason to shoot Barret. But Piers's first enquiries into the victim's business interests had produced nothing of interest. By aristocratic standards, he was not wealthy, but for a younger son he was comfortable enough, and had invested a little sensibly on the Exchange. He liked gaming but had no debts. And his only women appeared to be his wife and Annie Eastleigh.

Maybe they should be looking more closely at Mrs. Bootle's relationships, not just with her brother-in-law. Her only family might feel insulted by Barret's open infidelity... Although that was doubtful. Few men of his rank and wealth remained entirely faithful to their wives. The most that could be hoped for, in general, was consideration and discretion.

Piers shuddered with distaste and prepared to observe. April should already be in the house, mixing with the permanent and temporary servants, hopefully without being discovered to be neither.

April. He did not want to remember yesterday evening. He had been so sure she would never go back, because he had forbidden it and because she really did not want to. But he had forgotten her courage and her loyalty.

Even when he knew she was missing, he had not suspected her of being there, not even when he had waited up to scold her unmercifully. But when she had come in, stinking of the place, with apparent bruises on her face...

It was probably funny. But he still could not laugh. He didn't underestimate what it had cost her to go, and he suspected she had read much of his fear and his care in his face. Yet she had still made him hot chocolate and they had drunk it together as friends.

One day she would stop surprising him. But he doubted it would be today. Entering Kinsley House, he crossed his fingers.

The house was still subdued, the entrance hall and public rooms swathed in black crepe. Occasional vases of lilies were the only decoration and seemed more oppressive to Piers than anything else. The heavy scent reminded him of too many other such occasions: the deaths of his parents, his brother, his cousins, his uncle. The chill of loss seeped into his bones.

The ladies of the house, Lady Kinsley and Mrs. Bootle, wore unrelieved black and welcomed their guests with suitable gravity. Piers murmured words of sympathy, sincere and yet sounding trite and inadequate to his own ears. He moved further into the room.

The first person he saw was his aunt, looking regal and sombre. Standing beside her were Gussie and Louise Austen. Since Haggs and Percy materialized on either side of him, Aunt Hortensia did not greet him with her usual accusations or complaints, merely sniffed by way of acknowledgement, and spoke politely to his companions.

Gussie was pleased to see him at least, although a faint, curiously defiant blush stained her cheeks as Haggard greeted her. Piers pretended not to notice and spoke to Louise instead.

"I'm pleasantly surprised to see you here, Miss Austen."

"Lord Dilworth invited us when we parted yesterday," she replied with a fleeting smile. "My aunt introduced me to yours."

A maid brushed past them, bearing a tray of sherry glasses which she offered to the group, head modestly down so that one saw mostly a starched white cap. While those who wished to took a glass from her tray, the cap moved and a pair of vital, deep blue eyes flashed up at him.

He took a glass himself without so much as a twitch of the lips. The maid moved on with her tray.

Louise said, "Was that...?"

"Indeed, but one doesn't notice servants, does one?"

She flushed, and seemed about to ask more questions when Lord Dilworth joined them.

"Lady Petteril," he said. "How kind of you to join us on this sad occasion."

"I could no less," Aunt Hortensia said with regal sorrow. "We are only just out of mourning ourselves and feel for your family's loss. You know my daughter, Augusta?"

Gussie and the rest of the group were greeted also, in hushed, gratingly insincere tones. Piers thought no less of him for that—one had to get through the public face of mourning somehow—though the speed with which he detached Louise Austen from the group was another matter.

"I know," Austen murmured, moving away with Piers and leaving Haggs to the tender mercies of Aunt Hortensia and Gussie. "You have not yet ruled him out."

"Even if he is innocent of the worst..." There was a limit to what he could say in this place, at this time without being overheard. Piers bit back the torrent of warnings and said only, "I would not let him near my cousin Gussie."

It did not have quite the effect he expected. Austen only grinned. "Don't worry. She still prefers you."

Piers had not even worked out the meaning of that when Barbara Bootle came up to them. They all murmured the platitudes expected of them, Mrs. Bootle with rather better grace than her brother-in-law. Her eyes seemed full, as though with tears, and Piers felt ashamed of his too-quick assumptions of her lack of grief. He of all people should understand its strange effects on different people.

"What will you do now?" Piers asked with more genuine sympathy of his own. Percy, answering a summons of his aunt's, had just excused himself. "Will you continue to make your home with Lord and Lady Kinsley?"

She shook her head in instant denial, even before less certain words came to her lips. "It is too early to think of such things. But perhaps I shall go to the country for a little, to my own family in Gloucestershire."

"Of course. The country can be soothing."

She glanced at him with curiosity. "Is that what you found? In your own grief?"

There was a very long answer he had no intention of giving. Instead, he smiled faintly. "Eventually."

"There are no easy answers, are there, my lord?"

"No," he agreed.

"Accusing the innocent does not help," she said shakily. "It was very gracious of Mr. Austen to come. And you, as his friend."

She moved away before he could respond, though not before he had seen the fullness of her eyes about to spill over.

He wanted away from this house very badly. Ashamed of his suspicions of the dead man's family, only the possibility that the real murderer was present, someone he had not even thought of, kept him in the room.

April brushed past him, muttering below her breath. "Straight in front with curly black hair. Horton."

Horton. One of Barret's friends who had been frequent visitor to the house in Kensington. Piers kept his gaze on the curls, eventually recalling that he had indeed spoken to the man at Gussie's ball. It was therefore quite easy to amble up as an acquaintance and insert himself into Horton's line of vision. He inclined his head to the group in general, every inch the aloof viscount.

Horton smiled at him, a lightening of his somewhat wan expression. "Petteril. Didn't know you were a friend of poor Bootle."

"I wasn't really." *Or at all, in fact.* Through the open door he saw April walking smartly across the hallway, in the opposite direction to the baize door. Had she gone to the dining room on some task? Or was she investigating? "Supporting my aunt," he added hastily to Horton, "who is a friend of Lady Kinsley."

"Good of you. I won't deny I feel the loss. The manner of it as much as anything."

"Shocking," Piers agreed. Horton was the first who had alluded to the murder in his hearing, and when he looked the man directly in the eye, he saw the misery of grief, the loss of a friend brought home by the day's proceedings. If there was guilt there, Piers could not discern it.

Horton seemed contented enough to draw apart with Piers, who murmured, "Who could have done such a thing?"

"God knows. Kinsley was blaming a fellow called Austen. Apparently the gun was his. But Dilworth's denying that. *He* thinks it was Mrs. Eastleigh."

But then Dilworth wanted Mrs. Eastleigh's house.

"Can't have been," Piers said. "She and her maid were together when the shot was fired."

"I couldn't have imagined it anyway. She was devoted to Barret."

"He must have made some enemy he shouldn't," Piers said. "Had a bit of a temper, I hear."

"He could rub people up the wrong way," Horton allowed. "But there was no malice in him. Anyone could see that. In any case, there's no excuse to *kill* the man."

"Absolutely not," Piers said. "Horrible for the family to deal with, too. How is Mrs. Bootle coping?"

"With dignity," Horton said ruefully.

"And Mrs. Eastleigh?" Piers asked on impulse.

Horton blinked, a hint of shame in his eyes. "I really don't know. I suppose someone should look in on her..." He glanced around him as though to be sure the mention of Barret's mistress in these hallowed halls had not been overheard.

Piers, following his gaze, saw Barbara Bootle leaving the room. Uneasily, he wondered where April was.

Chapter Nine

Having pointed Lord Petteril toward Mr. Horton—whose name she had happened to overhear while serving sherry—April wondered what to do next. The footmen in the drawing room were glaring at her as if she had no business to be there, which she hadn't, and she didn't really want to go back to the kitchen where she doubted she could learn anything more about the family.

She hastened toward the dining room, hoping to find people there, chattering, preferably Mrs. Bootle, or Lord Dilworth, or the other cove Petteril was interested in—Mr. Keyes, who had been to Annie's house several times, although no one knew of anything he had against Bootle, let alone against Percy Austen or Annie.

But there were only servants in there, rearranging dishes to suit the precise instructions of the lugubrious butler. Silently, April abandoned her empty tray just inside the room where one of the servants would notice it, and hastened along to the next door which was closed.

She pressed her ear to it, since the hall around her was empty. Then, hearing nothing within, she whisked herself inside and softly closed the door behind her. Her heart hammering, she glanced around a book-lined room. It was a little like Petteril's libraries both here in town and in Haybury Court, only smaller, and with more space between the elegant bookshelves. There were comfortable chairs and a dainty sort of a writing desk, but no solid work tables of the kind in the Petteril libraries.

Perhaps this was a study, though she wasn't perfectly sure what the difference was. She flitted across to the desk by the window and opened the first drawer—it was stuffed with bills, most of them unreceipted. They were all addressed to Lord Kinsley. If this was his room, it wasn't likely she would learn anything useful, but since she was here...

She closed the first and opened the second drawer, which seemed to contain more personal letters. However, before she could even touch one, a sudden shuffling sound by the door had her shoving the drawer shut and diving beneath the desk.

Someone came in. April heard a gasp, the rustle of a gown, and sliding feet, and then silence. Afraid to breathe, let alone move, April couldn't understand why no one was yet shouting at her in outrage. By some miracle, had she really not been seen from the door?

She risked shifting one foot, swivelled, and glanced over her shoulder. A couple stood just inside the door in a passionate embrace. With heartfelt gratitude, she shuffled toward the curtain behind the desk, and slipped behind it into the window embrasure.

Safe. Still safe.

"Let me go, Thomas," the woman gasped. "This is madness here, at *this* moment of all others..."

"I know. But you need strength from somewhere."

Interesting. These weren't servants seizing a moment away from their duties. With a mere glimpse of black skirts and male legs, she hadn't been able to tell who had interrupted her. But those voices belonged to nobs. And there came an expensive rustle of silk as they moved further into the room, allowing her another glimpse of black skirts. Impossible to tell who they belonged to.

"Is it very awful?" the man asked ruefully.

April eased herself upright, so that she now stood behind the curtain, and this gave her a much better view. She could see the gentleman, although she had no idea who he was. The lady, with her back to April, could have been anyone.

"I could scream," the lady admitted. "I must get out of this house. The worst of it is, I *am* sad that Barret is dead." She swung around to him, her expression anguished, and April saw with excitement that it was Barbara Bootle, Barret's widow.

"Of course you are. Even I am. He was not a bad man, just not worthy of you. Be strong for another few days, my love. Then go to the country and I will follow."

She touched her forehead to his shoulder. "You are my only strength, Thomas... But I have to go. My absence will be noticed,"

Another kiss, more hurried, and the widow rushed away out of April's view. The door opened and closed with a small click.

In the silence, April was afraid to breathe in case he heard it. *Go now*, she willed him. *Quickly before everyone pours into the dining room...*

He sighed and sat down on the sofa behind him.

April cast her eyes to the ceiling. She wondered if she could get out of the window. She positively itched to share this discovery with Lord Petteril. It changed everything if the widow had a lover. One of them must have done Barret in, though why they had to blame it on Austen or Annie was beyond her.

Well, actually, it wasn't beyond anyone. Annie was beloved by Barbara's husband. while Barbara had been trapped by convention here in his parents' house. She must have hated Annie. It wasn't really so surprising that she had lashed out. She might even have taken this Thomas as her lover for revenge—at least in the first place, whatever she felt now. And if she married him in a year or two, no one would bat an eyelid. Barbara was free.

But which of them had croaked Barret to make her so?

April's nose began to tickle. On the sofa, Thomas sighed and rubbed his forehead. Did he look like a guilty man? He certainly looked like a troubled one. His shoulders were rounded, his expression bleak.

Barbara was saddened to some degree at least by Barret's death. Or said she was. It could be guilt.

Did either of them know what the other had done?

A chill of fear shivered up April's spine. She was, probably, the only other person who knew about this affair. And she was alone, where she had no business being, with the likely murderer.

She breathed in too rapidly, and her nose tickled with more urgency. She was going to sneeze.

Desperately, she wiggled her nose, trying to will the sneeze away, at the same time as praying for Thomas to leave the room.

If he came straight toward her, she could, probably, dive out the other side of the curtain, and bolt out the door before he caught her. She was used to that kind of manoeuvre. It had saved her a thrashing or worse on several occasions over the years. The sneeze rushing on her was inevitable now.

The door opened so suddenly that she jumped. So did Thomas, leaping off the sofa. Voices drifted in from the hallway, mostly Lord Petteril's saying, "Do you think so? I have always believed the opposite."

"What, that we should educate the masses?" came another voice in apparent disbelief. She didn't know that voice, but neither was coming any closer. More to the point, her sneeze had been frightened off.

"Shall we take a little nourishment?" suggested the fading voice that was not Petteril's. "It might make each other's views more palatable. Have you..."

Thomas hastened toward the door and a second later, April heard it click shut.

She breathed out into the blessed silence and stepped warily around the curtain. She crossed the empty room at speed and pressed her ear to the door. She could hear one or two subdued voices, a few people moving quietly between the drawing room and the dining room where the buffet had been set up. *Damn.* But unless one of the Bootles saw her, no one else would notice a servant.

Would they?

She risked it, walking out as if she had every reason in the world to have been in the room, and hurried across the mostly empty hall toward the green baize door to the kitchen. She saw no one she knew, except Louise Austen, loitering in the drawing room doorway, watching her.

April risked a quick grin as she passed, then immediately straightened her face. Time to scarper.

Louise, doing her best to be a modestly behaved young lady in a gathering where she felt acutely uncomfortable, found her attention too frequently drawn to the enigmatic Lord Petteril. Because of that, she saw him noticing April leave the drawing room with her empty tray.

Louise knew he was looking into the possibilities of one of Barret Bootle's own family or friends shooting him. That was why April was here, pretending to be a servant hired for the occasion. And why, no doubt, Petteril was keeping a subtle eye on her. The girl was not even a natural servant. She couldn't be subservient if she tried. Louise rather admired that, but the fact that Petteril looked out for her made her admire him all the more.

And yet she could not quite like it.

Therefore, when he strolled out of the room, she murmured something to her aunt about the cloakroom, and also left the room. So did several other people, because apparently the buffet luncheon was available.

Petteril had fallen into conversation with an elderly gentleman in the hallway, and they were strolling as they talked. She could not tell which of them initiated the pause outside the closed door next to the dining room, but she definitely saw Petteril's fidgeting hand grasp the door handle behind him and push as he spoke.

Then the pair strolled on toward the dining room and vanished from her view. Reluctantly, Louise moved on toward the cloakroom. She would rather have joined Lord Petteril in the dining room and demanded to know what he was up to. If she had, she would not have observed the gentleman emerging like a startled fawn from the door Petteril had opened.

On impulse, she drifted back toward the drawing room, trying to remember the man's name. And from the doorway, she saw April slip out of the same room and hurry toward the back of the house. The girl even flashed Louise a smile that would have been insolent and vulgar if it had not been so wretchedly dazzling.

But it wasn't the girl's unusual beauty that depressed her. It was the feeling that she and Lord Petteril were acting together, that he had known she was in that room and that his pushing it open had been some kind of signal to her, or perhaps a warning to the other man to leave her alone.

As though she had conjured him up, Lord Petteril walked out of the dining room with a plate, and immediately saw her skulking in the drawing room doorway. Perhaps she should finally go to the cloakroom. Except that he smiled as he came toward her and she seemed to be paralyzed,

"Care to share?" he said, offering his plate.

She didn't want anything, but she took a small pastry, just to keep him with her. "Thank you." She lowered her voice. "What are you up to, my lord? I just saw your April come out of the room across the hall." Was that relief in his face?

"I don't suppose you saw anyone else go in or out?"

"I saw the man who was in there with her. He came out before she did."

Petteril's eyes focused on hers and quite suddenly she saw something far more than the kindness and amiability that lurked behind his frequently aloof manners. It was not simply intelligence, that was too vague. It was something so incisive, so cuttingly perceptive that she was almost afraid. Except, of course, that his interest was not in her.

"Do you know him?" Lord Petteril asked.

"Keyes," she said, recalling the man's name, at last. "Mr. Thomas Keyes."

Lord Petteril smiled.

Back at Petteril House, April, who had been pacing up and down the library floor, desperate for his lordship to come back, had to stop herself from dragging him inside when he eventually opened the door and sauntered in.

"She's got a lover and his name is Thomas," she said triumphantly.

"Thomas Keyes."

She knew her face fell. She had wanted to impress him. Foolishly. "You already know."

He wandered past her to his favourite chair and threw himself into it, crossing one ankle over his knee. "I found out his name from Miss Austen, that's all."

"It was you rattled the door?"

"I had a feeling you were in there. And yet it was Mrs. Bootle who came out, not you. Where did you hide?"

"Under the desk, and then behind the curtain. I nearly died when they came in, but they weren't paying me no attention. I could have danced a jig around them and they wouldn't have noticed. Definitely lovers. I think he done it. Croaked Barret to marry her. And if he's Thomas Keyes, that's one of the coves Annie knows, who came round the house a lot and might have found the pistol. Maybe that's even why he went so often—he can't have had much love for Barret, after all—just waiting for his chance to do him in."

"It's certainly interesting, isn't it? Likeliest."

She was watching him carefully. Slowly, she walked across and crouched down at his feet, leaning back on her heels. "You don't believe it."

"I *could* believe it," he said. "It all fits. Like a bad play. Life is usually...messier than that."

She blinked. "You want it to be Dilworth because he likes Miss Austen."

Although a faint flush crept into his cheeks, he actually laughed. "I might believe she could do better than Dilworth, but I wouldn't have him hanged just to spoil his chances with her. No, if I want it to be anyone it's Jason Marr. Only it can't be, can it?"

"Like you said, life is messier than that."

"Sometimes, I am staggered by my own cleverness."

Guilt swamped Barbara Bootle like a fever. What Barret had done was no excuse for what she did. And yet she could not regret it. She only hoped the terrible guilt would fade in time, in the peace, perhaps, of her old home in Gloucestershire.

In the meantime, she concentrated on getting through the next excruciating meal at Kinsley House, agreeing with her father-in-law that there had been an excellent turn out for Barret's memorial, and that it was a great comfort that he would be remembered so fondly by so many.

It wasn't, of course. Nothing had comforted Barbara except the feel of Thomas's arms around her, and even then, the guilt had made her imagine they were being watched.

Somehow, she got through the meal and the requisite half hour sewing in the drawing room with her silently bereaved mother-in-law before the gentlemen re-joined them and she felt able to abandon them all and go to her own bedchamber.

She could have screamed when Toby followed her out of the room, and even up the staircase.

"Are you quite well, Barbara?" he asked anxiously.

"Quite," she said, trying not to speak between her teeth. She swallowed. "Just a headache, which I'm sure will pass if I can only sleep."

"I'm sure Mama will have a powder that might help."

"Oh, I have some of my own. I just need rest." She forced a smile. "Thank you for your concern, Toby. But I think your parents need you more."

He ignored the last, turning along the passage with her. "Mama tells me you are thinking of going to Gloucestershire."

"Indeed. I think I would like to be with my own mother for a little."

Toby nodded. "Understandable. And probably for the best."

She opened her sitting room door, but when she turned to say goodnight, somehow he was already in the room. Her lips tightened. She wanted to throw him out immediately, and yet he had said, *"Probably for the best."*

"What do you mean?" she asked.

"Mmm?" He was looking around her sitting room, which was more than Barret ever had. "Oh, only that I shall of course look out for your interests while you are away. We all shall."

"My interests? What on earth are they?"

"Don't be naive, Barbara," Toby said with the patience one used to a slow child. "Barret was shot and Papa will not let it go unpunished. If it was not That Woman, then they will look further and more carefully."

The blood drained from her face. She and Toby had told the magistrate that, having returned from different evening parties, they had met in the drawing room just before midnight and talked there for about half an hour. Of course, it was not true.

He smiled without mirth, holding her gaze like a light held a startled deer's. She knew suddenly how that deer felt.

"Don't worry. No one could possibly suspect you," he said, his eyes releasing her at last.

Then why did we lie? Just to avoid unpleasantness. It had been instinctive. But looked at with the eyes of the law, either she or Toby could have killed Barret and lied to cover it. She laid her hand on the back of a chair to steady herself, then snatched it away when she realized it was shaking.

Toby picked up the tiny Italian statue from the table. "I don't suppose Petteril has been asking you questions, has he?"

"Lord Petteril?" she said, frowning. "What sort of questions?"

"Oh, about Barret and the murder and where we all were when it happened."

"Of course not! Why would you even imagine such a thing?"

"Well, seems he likes to stick his somewhat supercilious nose into other people's business. He made the Gadsbys go and ruralize rather than live in London, you know. Spoiled little Gussie Withan's marriage hopes with a perfectly eligible parti, and had Bertie packed off to a fighting regiment in Spain."

Barbara had difficulty imagining the aloof if mild-mannered viscount exerting himself to such a degree of either action or malice. "What makes you believe all that?"

"Had it from Lady Petteril herself. She dislikes him cordially."

"So it would appear."

"On the other hand, I also heard from quite a different source that he personally pursued the perpetrator of some murder committed down at Haybury Court, his country seat. Got the fellow, too, leaving a trail of destruction behind him."

"I don't see how this is any concern of mine," she said impatiently. "Or yours. Now, I am—"

"Don't you? He is asking questions about Barret, you know. Sticking his nose into *our* affairs, and I doubt he'll stop just because he noticed some pistol balls that apparently make it impossible—or at least extremely unlikely—that either That Woman or Percy Austen could have done it. Austen is his friend, of course, but he also seems to be taking That Woman's part."

"I don't see why." Barbara just wanted him to go away.

"No, neither do I. I tried to get her house back for you—even just for the rent—but she sent her solicitor to read Barret's will and scuppered it. Turns out her solicitor is also Petteril's. As I say, he interferes."

"Why are you telling me all this?" she asked, distressed.

"So that you know I have every reason in the world to look out for your interests," he said laying down the exquisite statue and walking at last toward the open door. "As I know now you will look out for mine. Wherever you are."

Chapter Ten

Piers was not terribly sure whether or not he had met Thomas Keyes, either during his earlier sojourn in London or at Gussie's ball. He could not recall hearing the name before Annie mentioned it, though that meant nothing. Confronted by seas of strangers' faces, names were the least of his worries.

Discovering where Keyes lived was not difficult. Having sent April to see what else she could discover about him from Annie, Piers drove his curricle and greys around to Cavendish Square, where he paid a lad to look after them while he went inside. He had never had the heart to employ another tiger for the purpose, in case it upset April.

Having presented his card, Piers was shown almost at once into the breakfast parlour, where Mr. Keyes rose to greet him. He was a pleasant looking man perhaps a year or two under forty, with short, fair hair and a surprised expression. He rose from the table to say, "Good morning, Lord Petteril. Join me for breakfast? Coffee?"

"Coffee would be most welcome. Thank you."

While the servant poured him a cup and silently departed, Piers sat down to one side of Keyes.

"Sorry to disturb you so early," he said, "I know it is shockingly ill-mannered, but I was afraid they would be gone."

Keyes looked confused, as indeed he should. "Gone?"

"The horse."

"What horse?"

Piers set down his cup. "You are selling a bay hunter?" he asked uncertainly.

Keyes grinned. "Sadly not. I don't even possess such an animal."

Piers struck himself in the forehead. "Then I don't even have a reason for my rudeness. How unforgiveable!"

Keyes laughed. "Not at all. You have clearly mixed me up with someone else. I know Barrowfield is selling a hunter, but not sure he's up to your height."

"It can't have been him then. Percy Austen definitely approved this beast for me."

"Hmm..." Keyes showed no reaction to Austen's name, but then Austen himself knew of no enmity between them.

After an agreeable and even amusing five minutes talking about horses and their owners and the likelihood of their being the one sought by Piers, the door opened and a young girl of seventeen or so came in. She wore a pristine morning gown of palest blue.

"Good morning, Papa. Oh!" She paused at the unexpected sight of a stranger at the breakfast table.

Piers rose and bowed while Keyes introduced them. "My daughter Amanda. Amanda, are you acquainted with Lord Petteril?"

"We have not been introduced," the young lady replied with a charming smile. She even blushed a little. "Though I saw you at Miss Withan's ball. You are her cousin, are you not?"

"I have that felicity. How do you do, Miss Keyes?"

"I am supposed to be bored or exhausted, aren't I? In fact, I'm having a wonderful time, dancing until three in the morning and sleeping until... Well, until now! I'd have been up for hours at home in Gloucestershire."

Gloucestershire? Was that not where Mrs. Bootle's family lived? They had probably known each other for some time.

Piers stayed only another ten minutes or so, long enough to see the easy affection between the father and daughter, and to find it increasingly difficult to imagine Thomas Keyes shooting someone in the head and then planting the duelling pistol beside the body. Apart from anything else, why, even in a moment of lovesick madness, would he take such a risk of leaving his daughter ruined and unprotected?

An ugly suspicion popped into his head. Could Barret have known of the affair with his wife and threatened him in some way? He didn't want to think so, but as he climbed back into his curricle, and tossed the boy a coin for looking after the horses, he knew he couldn't yet rule it out. He hoped April could learn from Annie whether or not Barret knew about Keyes, because he had no idea how he could possibly set about asking Barbara Bootle herself.

No, he would have to speak to Keyes again, in private, when his daughter was not present. Unless he could prove before then where Keyes was at the time of the murder. He drove through the park and on to Kensington, where he found April and Annie conversing with some hilarity in what April called "nob accents."

"I'll bet you a shilling you can't keep it up until we leave," he said, sitting astride one of the upright chairs and resting his arm along its back. "Annie, did Barret know about Barbara's affair with Keyes?"

"Ape's just asked me the same question. If he did know, he didn't tell me. To be honest, I don't think he'd have begrudged her."

"Even if they had a child?" April asked.

Annie considered. "He'd probably have accepted it. It might not be right, but he just wasn't *interested* in Barbara. Dilworth is the one who would have complained."

"Do you think Dilworth *did* know?" Piers asked quickly.

"Even if he did," April said, "it's hardly a motive to croak his brother."

"It's a poor one," Piers agreed.

"You still prefer Dilworth to Keyes as the killer?"

Piers sighed. "I like Keyes better. Doesn't make him innocent."

April turned to Annie, jerking her head back toward Piers. "He's annoyed 'cause it can't be Jace. Oh, he was here again. Annie paid him."

Piers frowned. The sting of alarm in his stomach kept him from looking at April. "You owe me a shilling," he pointed out, and to Annie, "When was he here?"

"First thing. He was gone before Ape arrived." Annie said, wrinkling her nose. "I won't deny it leaves me short. I wish I could see a way to make him bugger off."

"We'll think of something," Piers said vaguely. Mostly, he was relieved April hadn't had to face Jason Marr.

Sitting beside him on the journey home, April's hands fidgeted together. At last, she said, "I can't drive 'em in town, can I?"

He shook his head apologetically. "Maids don't drive their masters. Nor ride horses in the park, sadly." He had begun to teach her to ride at Haybury Court and she had thoroughly enjoyed it. He felt guilty introducing her to pastimes she couldn't practice when she chose.

"Do assistants?" she asked.

"I don't know. I've never come across anyone with a female assistant. But it would certainly cause all the kind of talk we wish to avoid." He turned along the road rather than through the park this time. "I was thinking, though, once we've sorted this out, I need to go to Sussex. And to Yorkshire."

"You got land all over the place."

"I know. And I'd like to return to Haybury Court in the autumn if not before."

"Will you need me to look over the houses?" she asked casually.

"Of course. In fact, I don't think there's even a housekeeper in Sussex, though there is definitely a house." Even as he said the words, he knew he was digging a deeper hole for her, putting her in a position where suspicion could damage her. There had just never seemed to be any other options. She could never have been a proper maidservant, but what the devil was he making her into? Perhaps it really was time he sent her to Lady Haggard, who had offered to take her in, in whatever capacity she wished. Yes, they would call on her in Sussex *en route*, and with luck he could leave April there with her.

The thought caused an empty chasm to open in his chest and in his mind. He would miss her far too much, which was only another reason for her to go. But the main reason was for her own sake, and for that, he could make himself do it.

He turned deliberately back to the murder. "Barbara Bootle and Lord Dilworth told the same tale of talking together at home when Barret died. I have always wondered if they are lying, and if so, how to get one or the other to admit it."

"Tricky, when you have no authority to ask," April said in such perfect accents that he said, "I won't take that shilling from you after all."

They were both silent for most of the rest of the journey, until as they drew up to Petteril House, April said, "There's another carriage. You got visitors."

"It's my aunt's carriage," he said. More properly, it was his, but since she had taken it, he chose not to take it back.

"She going to tell you off again?"

"Inevitably."

"Tell her to sling her hook. Worked the last time."

“So it did. But actually, I might pick her brains a little more about the whereabout of all our suspects on the night Barret died.”

“Think she might have seen some of ’em?”

“Someone must have.”

April was already at the horses’ heads, so Piers left her there to run up the steps to the house.

“I gather my aunt is here,” he said to Park, who opened the door to him.

“Oh, no, sir. Your cousin. She’s in the drawing room.”

In better humour, Piers ran up to the drawing room to find his cousin gazing out of the window onto the street.

“Maria?” he said in surprise. “I thought you’d gone back to the—”

It was not Maria’s face but Gussie’s that turned to him. He was familiar enough with them now to recognize her easily. And she was laughing.

“No, just me! It’s the hat that tricked you.”

Something seemed to fizz in his brain and melted away when he reached for it. “The hat,” he repeated, frowning.

“The hat was Maria’s,” she explained. “She gave it to me before she left London. It rather suits me, don’t you think? Adds some maturity and solemnity.”

He regarded the frivolous confection. “No, it doesn’t do that, but it does suit you. What can I do for you?”

“Mama has sent me to ask you to escort us to the Braithwaite ball. With Jeremy and Bertie both gone, you’re the best escort we have left.”

Piers answered something and let her prattle on, while he thought of hats and tried to think why his brain had responded as it had. He rummaged about in his mind for some time without success, and then suddenly he remembered.

“Hat!” he exclaimed, in the middle of Gussie’s story.

Gussie blinked rapidly. “I beg your pardon?”

He leapt to his feet, and unceremoniously pulled his cousin to hers. “If I’m still in town, of course I shall escort you to the ball. But you have to go home now.”

“Why? Mama does not expect me for another half hour.”

“I have to go out.”

“Why?” she challenged, inclined to dig her heels in.

"I have to see a man about a hat," Piers said, tugging the bell rope on his way past. "Goodbye, Gussie!"

Jimmy Knott, the Bow Street Runner, was discovered in the magistrate's house and was happy enough to talk about Jason Marr and his hat.

"You recognized him that night in the tavern in Finnegan Lane—the Ratter, did you call it?—because of his hat," Piers said.

"Well, yes, but I was sitting next to the door. I saw his face, too."

"When he came in? Then you were there first?"

"Yes, and yes."

"Did he know you were there?"

Knott considered. "Yes. I'm usually there on a Monday, 'cause I know *he* is. He never looked at me, but his thugs did. That Jerry Nash for one. Frankie Sullivan for another. And Big Leeky. They'll have told him I was there if he didn't see for hisself. They made sure to sit right at the back where I couldn't hear them."

"And Jason Marr kept his hat on all evening? Never took it off?"

"Not that I saw. There were crowds of people between us now and again, but I always saw the hat."

"And he never moved all night, you said? Not even to relieve himself of all that ale he must have been swigging?"

Knott thought back. "Yes, he went out the back once. But he were only gone a minute."

"Wearing the hat?"

"Of course."

"Were you still there when he left the tavern?"

"I was. And yes, the damned hat was still on his head. With his face beneath it."

"Was there ever a time," Piers asked carefully, "when someone else could have been wearing it?"

"No," Knott scoffed. "He wouldn't let anyone else wear it. Like his crown, that hat is."

"He knew you were there, watching and listening," Piers pursued. "What if he wanted to play a trick on you? Go out the back, for example and send one of his men, this Nash or Sullivan, back in wearing the hat."

Knott stared at him. "While he went to the Queen's Head and conducted business that would hang him, or at least transport him?"

"Or to Kensington to murder Barret Bootle. When did he go out the back?"

Knott scratched his head. "About ten? Half past? And he left the Ratter with his cronies at nearly two in the morning."

"Then he had time to do it and come back to let you see him leave. Wearing the hat again."

"It's a bit of a stretch, isn't it? Why'd Marr kill this nob anyway?"

"Because the nob was keeping a lady friend who used to be one of Marr's girls. I hear times are hard for him, and he wanted her back to restore a little more class to the Queen's Head. By planting the pistol from this lady's house, he hoped to implicate her, make her desperate to escape."

"And up steps Marr to the rescue, offering to hide her in St. Giles—for a price. Hasn't happened yet, though, has it?"

"No, she's not desperate enough. I think he underestimates her determination to stay away. And the fact that her previous lover was blamed instead of her. And now they're both exonerated. I think Jason Marr did it."

Knott's face showed a bizarre mixture of hope and scorn. "I think he did a lot of things. In fact, I know it and I can't prove any of 'em. You can't prove this either, can you?"

"Not yet," Piers admitted. "But it makes sense. Aren't there private rooms, or corners in the Ratter tavern where they could have hidden from you?"

"Well, yes," Knott admitted.

"But they didn't. They wanted you to see the hat, but not be close enough to be aware when it was on a different head."

Knott drew himself up to his full height. "They made use of me? *Me?*"

"It's possible. He seems a cheeky enough fellow to me. And as you say, nothing has ever touched him. He's got away with murder before in St. Giles. He thinks he can get away with killing gentlemen too."

"They're all souls, wherever they're born," Knott said austerely.

"I agree. But if they hang him for one, he's hanged for them all."

Knott's eyes cleared. "What do you want to do?"

Chapter Eleven

Jason Marr was in a foul mood. Annie Eastleigh had paid up this morning with loud complaints but absolutely no visible fear. He'd hoped to be in possession of her house by now and earning good, legal rent, while she herself drew the richer clientele away from the unspeakable Ells woman and back to the Queen's Head. Spoke like a lady now, Annie did. There were men, low and rough but with plenty of the readies, who'd pay good money for that voice whispering in their ear. And if she brought a couple of her actress friends into the game...

He pounded his fist on the table, making the dog snouting about the floor, start and poise itself to bolt.

Bloody fantasy. He hadn't even got *Annie* where he wanted her, never mind others like her. And that hurt—not just his pocket or his reputation, but the same place that hurt when Annie had left him in the first place.

And now he was sure scum like Lord the prig and Tatty the fence, were diddling him, only he couldn't prove it. Lord sat beside him now, and he knew the bastard was lying. He thought about taking him into one of the back rooms and getting Frankie to give him a warning. Or Leeky to make it permanent. Would that show others he was still tough? Or just reveal to everyone that Lord had felt able to lower his dues? When did life start getting so bleeding difficult?

But no, it wasn't difficult at all. Lord was no loss to Jace's empire. Another thief would just take his place, one duly frightened of Captain Jace. He opened his mouth to give Leeky the order, just as a tall man walked in off the street. He wore a slightly battered high-crowned beaver hat and spectacles that glinted in the brief shaft of sunlight that followed him through the door and then vanished.

Beside him, Lord swore beneath his breath. His mouth twisted into something like a snarl and his eyes spat malevolence.

Jace turned and regarded the newcomer with considerably more interest. He was a stranger, a man with an ingratiating smile and hard, watchful eyes. He carried a stick that Jace suspected concealed a blade, and there were old ink stains on his cuffs, fresh ones on his long, clever fingers.

A forger, Jace suspected, and from his manner, probably a good one.

"Afternoon, gents," this stranger said amiably to Jace and Lord who were both staring at him, and to Finn behind the counter, "Ale, if you please."

He sounded not so much like a nob fallen on hard times, but like someone who'd lived among them and studied them well enough to ape their speech.

"You got some nerve swanning in here," Lord growled.

The stranger glanced over his shoulder and around the room, noting Jace, Frankie, Jerry, Leeky, and back to Lord. "Me? Oh, no."

"Introduce us," Jace commanded.

Lord smiled wolfishly. "With pleasure. This here is Captain Jace. Cap'n, this is the lowlife what stole my 'prentice."

"What 'prentice?" Jace demanded.

"Ape. Cheeky little lad."

Jace vaguely remembered the skinny little article who hung around with Lord sometimes. Ran errands for a crust or a coin, like a thousand urchins in the city. Lord used him to get into houses through small spaces.

"Must be a different Ape," the stranger said, nodding his thanks to Finn the potman. "*My* Ape didn't learn anything from you except some choice words that would have made even my mother blush."

Jace began to like him. He was certainly putting Lord in his place, and Lord was getting far too big for his prigged boots. Perhaps this was more amusing than simply garrotting him.

"You got a name, Mr. Lowlife?" Jace mocked.

The forger took a healthy swallow of ale. "I do. But you can call me..." He smiled. "Quill."

Lord snorted and muttered something about calling him exactly what he liked.

"And what brings you to this fine establishment, Mr. Quill?" Jace enquired. "Something tells me you are not a man for random visits."

"I rarely have the time, Captain. I am a man who needs to work."

Jace caught the eye of the girl lurking on the stairs—she called herself Jemima—and jerked his head. Obediently, she hurried down, caught the direction of his gaze, and began swinging her hips as she strutted toward the stranger.

Jace smiled at him, baring his teeth. "All work and no play, Mr. Quill, is bad for any man."

Jemima, leaned her plump arm on Quill's shoulder. He didn't look surprised. He even smiled at her, although he blushed like a schoolgirl.

"Sadly, I am a very dull man," Quill said. He actually patted the girl's arm. "Though I will happily buy the lady a drink."

"I'll have a glass o' gin," Jemima said at once.

Finn, scowling, was obliged to fetch her one. She removed her arm from Quill's shoulder, but stayed closed to him, smiling up at him. He smiled back.

"Work brings you to this establishment in the middle of the day?" Jace asked with a hint of a sneer. He pushed his hat further to the back of his head.

Frankie and Jerry both grinned. Even Lord looked pleased.

Quill dragged his gaze away from Jemima. "The prospect of it does. I have been speaking with some lesser persons in the area, including Mrs. Ells around the corner."

"Oh?" Jace said coldly. "Bet you didn't learn much."

Frankie and Jerry laughed.

"Oh, but I did," Quill assured them seriously. "I learned that the good lady has neither the breadth of vision nor the resources that might require a... scribe of my abilities. Nor the wit to expand into new markets."

"What's he talking about?" Lord demanded.

"About the Captain here," Quill answered in apparent surprise. "I have decided that you, sir, are the only man in the area worthy of my talents."

"The only man in London?" Jace said with derision. He liked flattery as well as the next man, but it needed to be believable and he was far from sure compliments from this cove were worth anything.

Quill's teeth flashed. They were very fine and white. "Hardly. I am fortunate enough to have clients and connections all over the city, but until recent days I had not seen much potential in St. Giles."

"Being too busy mixing with the nobs," Lord jeered.

"Oh, the nobs don't mix with me, Mr. Lord," Quill said. "But some have the foresight to make use of my talents."

Jace looked from Quill to Lord. "How do you know each other? You've never mentioned him to me."

Lord looked furtive. "Told you," he growled. "He prigged my 'prentice. God knows why. Bleeding useless little article."

"Not in my hands," Quill said modestly.

Jemima suddenly slammed her glass on the counter. "Here. If that's where your tastes lie and you touch one hair of Ape's—"

"Shut it," Jace commanded, and she lapsed into glaring silence.

Quill looked down his disdainful nose at her. "I never touch the staff, my own or anyone else's and you, girl, have a filthy mind."

"Goes with the job, dunnit?" Jemima retorted and Quill unexpectedly clinked his glass against hers on the counter. She picked it up again.

Quill looked around Jace's men and Lord. He presented no possible threat, and yet there was something about the eyes, the posture... Jace had a notion they had met before, only he couldn't for the life of him recall where. That made him feel wrong-footed, too. He was glad of the other men's presence, for prestige as well as comfort. He was glad also of the others keeping watch around the outside of the house, though for officers of the law more than would-be rivals in crime.

Quill said, "You must have need of a good...clerk, Captain."

"What, to write everything down for the constables?" Jerry said. He tapped his head. "Everything's kept up here."

"Oh, very few people want to keep an account of everything they do," Quill said impatiently. He took a bit of pencil and a folded piece of paper from his pocket and spread them on the counter. The paper was blank. "A man needs imagination, not records for posterity. And when that imagination requires documents, then a scribe of my abilities is indispensable. Documents, you see, are most necessary to the man of business, proof before the law of the land. They can make you a master of property, a father, an inheritor. They can make all your legal problems go away and make you rich beyond your wildest dreams."

Despite the ignorant hooting of his oafs, Jace felt a surge of excitement. This could well be exactly what he needed, not just to revive his fortunes but to surpass them. He could even keep Annie in that same damned house.

"Call a spade a spade, Mr. Quill," Jace said, looking him in the eye—or at least in the spectacles, which seemed to wink whatever light came in the grubby window right back at him. "You're a forger."

"A scribe," Quill said gently. While he held Jace's gaze, his hand—long and thin and quick—was whisking over a corner of the paper. He glanced down at it, then back up. "And I have room for one more client. If you do. Would you care to discuss opportunities?"

"You don't know him," Jerry warned.

"Toss him out," Lord said with contempt.

A tiny smile played about Quill's lips. He glanced down at the paper again, made a couple of quick strokes with his pencil and pushed the paper in front of Jace.

Unhurriedly Jace glanced down. And laughed. The man had drawn a detailed picture of his hat, shading it so that light seemed to shine from the buckle. "Very pretty," Jace allowed. "But not very useful!" He snatched the pencil from Quill's loose fingers and beneath the hat, wrote his own name with a flourish.

Jace could read and write a little. Once, he had thought it gave him the edge over would be rivals, but truthfully, in brothel keeping and extortion, there wasn't a great deal of call for such a skill. Quill was right. He'd been thinking too small. Apart from the plan to own Annie's house. That was still good and could be built on. If this forger was any good.

"Copy that," Jace challenged, shoving the paper back with the pencil on top.

Quill picked up the pencil and, appearing to study and write at the same time, produced an identical signature in less time than it had taken Jace to write it in the first place. Jace began to smile.

"Jerry, write your name," Jace commanded.

For the next few minutes, everyone in the bar wrote their name or made their mark, and beneath them, the forger reproduced them exactly, including badly formed, shaky letters, the slope of the words, and the exact force used in making the crosses on the paper. A couple of men from the back drifted inside to watch and have their own writing copied, probably those who should have been on watch, for Quill was quite the performer, a showman in his own way, and Jace was inclined to grant him leeway.

"That's the easy part," Quill said modestly. "Anyone can forge a signature with practice, and even steal the ones you need to learn to copy. The real art is in making official documents that look like they're printed. Letterheads and such, seals and stamps. Got anything printed in here?"

Jace frowned in consternation. "This ain't an establishment of learning," he said sarcastically.

"Indeed not. Something engraved then?"

Tatty had taken stuff away barely an hour ago, including a very cleverly engraved bracelet.

Jace smiled and put his hand in his pocket, closing his fingers around the sleeve button and caressing it. It seemed to have brought him luck after all. He brought it out slowly and passed it in front of the forger's face. The initials engraved on the front were an intricate *BB*.

Piers did not get the chance to lift his eyes from Barret Bootle's cuff link before it vanished back into Jason Marr's coat pocket. His heart pounded so hard it seemed to be in his throat, and he had the insane urge to simply grab the button from Jace and bolt.

Instead, his pencil began, almost of its own volition to draw the two Bs he had glimpsed. The cuff link was passed beneath his eye again, showing one word on the reverse, "Anne", which he also wrote down, adding the elegant tail to the A that wound around the whole name in the shape of a heart.

Got you, Piers thought, more dazed than triumphant. But then, he still had to keep everyone absorbed so that the Bow Street Runners could approach and get into the building unseen. And he had no idea how long that would take.

"Jemima," Jace said, smiling. "Go and buy a newspaper. And you, Mr. Quill, oblige me by writing out something to look like a printed letterhead. And then the title deed to a property. Any property you like."

"Carlton House?" Piers suggested as the door swung shut behind Jemima. "Time Prinny was evicted."

Jace chortled. It even won a grin from his henchmen, though Lord was looking angrier and angrier.

Piers began with the firm's name: *Legit, Legit and Gottyer*, which raised another snigger. He wasn't making a particularly good job of it, for now that he knew where the proof was, his heart had gone out of the performance. Copying handwriting was a skill he had taught himself for fun as a boy, and it had certainly come in handy at school when he had written letters purporting to come from parents for himself and several others. He knew he was quick, but his art was nothing like good enough to be a professional forger.

Before anyone could notice, the door crashed open and Jemima shouted at the top of her voice, "The runners is coming! Some bastard brought 'em here!"

An instant, mad clattering came from above as the women upstairs ran out of their rooms and down the stairs.

"There's nothing here for them to find!" Marr shouted angrily. "Stop running around like headless chickens!"

Someone who looked vaguely familiar to Piers erupted from a back room. "They're round the back and all!"

Jace swore obscenely. "How'd they get so close?"

"'Cause those idiots you set to watch are all in here," Lord snarled, stabbing his finger at Piers. "Watching *him*! Now, who do you think brought the bleeding runners?"

A sudden shove from Jace's large hand sent Piers staggering backward into Frankie, who grabbed his arms from behind.

"What d'you really want?" Marr asked, ignoring the chaos breaking out around him. His eyes were hard and unafraid. Not even angry. He didn't think he had anything to fear.

Piers might have been sensibly afraid of a beating or a knife between the ribs. But the dangerous clerk he was portraying didn't care. He smiled. "What do I want? The sleeve button in your pocket, which you stole from Barret Bootle's body the night you murdered him."

Men fell through the front door, fighting. The women mostly ran screaming into the far corner; a couple flew at the runners, landing on their backs and yanking viciously on their hair. Even so, Marr's men were outnumbered by Knotts' runners.

Piers held Jace's stunned gaze, and kicked behind him, cracking Frankie's knee, then jerked forward so suddenly that Frankie was heaved off his feet, almost over Piers's shoulder. Freed in the chaos, Piers straightened to find himself facing not only Captain Jace, but the barrel of a wicked-looking pistol.

The one, no doubt, that had killed poor Barret Bootle.

His heart seemed to stop. *I'm dead. Now what will happen to April? To everyone? To the land in my care? What a stupid way to let everyone down...*

The pain in that was sharp yet curiously resigned. Only two months ago, he had tried to do this to himself. Now he had the certainty of death and wanted life with a force that shook him to the core. There was nothing he could do to prevent this. There was no hesitation and certainly no pity in Jason Marr.

Then the pistol swivelled, pointing instead at Jimmy Knott who was striding up to Marr with his club raised and the joy of a final victory on his face.

Piers didn't even think about it. He needed to live, but he couldn't let Knott die for him. He threw himself at Marr and they both went down with a roar that might have come from Piers or from the gun. White hot pain seared his flesh and his head struck the floor.

April had thought of an excellent ruse to persuade Barbara Bootle to tell the truth about her own and Dilworth's whereabouts at the time of Barret's murder. She barged into the library to tell Lord Petteril, remembering to knock on the door only after she was inside the room. Not that it mattered because he wasn't there.

She backed out again.

"Where's himself?" she asked Joshua, the first footman, who was crossing the landing from the dining room.

"Went out."

"Do you know where?" she asked, frowning.

"No," Joshua said repressively.

Francis, his underling, emerged from the servants' staircase, grinning. "He shouted something to Miss Withan about a hat."

"A hat?" She stared in Francis's direction without seeing him.

"In a tearing hurry he was. Looked very pleased with himself."

Jason Marr's hat? It was the only one she could think of relating to the murder, and she was sure only that would have got him so excited. Piqued that he had not taken her with him, or even told her what his discovery was, she turned away.

Everyone seemed to be obsessed with the damned hat. Not just Jace himself. She halted suddenly, her hand grasping for the balustrade.

He's gone to St. Giles. After Jace. Jesus, they'll kill him.

The footmen ignored her as she sank onto the step and grabbed her cap with both hands, pulling at it in an agonized effort to make herself think. After an instant, she sprang back up and bolted up the main staircase to the master's bedchamber. She knew exactly where it was, and pounded on the door—just in case he was still in there, which she willed him hard to be. The door was flung open, catapulting her inside, but there was no time for relief. It wasn't Lord Petteril who glared down at her but Stewart, his valet.

"Where is he?" she demanded.

"Out."

"When did he go?"

"Almost as soon as he got back."

"Oh God, that was hours ago... What did he take?"

Stewart could look damned supercilious when he wanted to. "That is not even my business, let alone yours."

"Please, Mr. Stewart, it's important," she pleaded. "Did he take a bag with old clothes in it?"

Stewart's face answered her though he said nothing.

She looked around wildly, and finding the desk by the window, she flew over and faster than she'd ever written anything legibly in her life before, she scribbled a few lines, hoping her spelling was up to the task, then folded the note and scrawled *Jimmy Knott, Bow Street Runner* on the outside. Then she straightened and rushed for the door.

Stewart seized her by the arm. She shook him off more from the need to hurry than from revulsion and shoved the note into his hand. "Make Francis take this immediately to Bow Street. His life depends on it."

Stewart didn't mistake the life concerned for Francis's. "Where is he? Where are you going?"

“The Queen’s Head in St. Giles.” After all, she’d promised Petteril she wouldn’t go again without telling someone. All the same, by the time she reached the front door, she wasn’t really surprised to find Stewart beside her.

At least he was useful at hailing hackneys. Inside, she regarded him doubtfully. At least he had not brought his hat, but his clothing was far too smart and expensive for the mean streets of St. Giles.

She threw him her cloak. “You’d better cover yourself with this. Wrong twig for where we’re going. Don’t open your mouth neither. Let me talk.”

He didn’t answer, though he did take the cloak.

She looked out of the window as though that would make the carriage move any faster. Stupidly, she corrected herself in a small voice. “Don’t open your mouth *either*.”

He might have smiled, but it was gone before she glanced at him again.

At least he didn’t hold her up but let her drag him through the noxious alleys and stairways to the Queen’s Head. A lot of people seemed to be heading smartly away from it. Others were drifting towards it from sheer curiosity. A stray dog she remembered loped past her in a hurry.

A knot of terrible fear dragged at her stomach.

“There’s a fight,” Stewart said grimly.

As one, they ran through the broken door of the Queen’s Head, and skidded to a halt.

April had seen countless such brawls, although not usually involving officers of the law, their red waistcoats inappropriately merry and bright amongst the brutality. She had always found a safe place to keep out of the way until it was all over and hadn’t cared much about the outcome. But this, this was her worst nightmare, etched like a vignette before her eyes.

Captain Jace, still in his damned hat, stood curiously aloof, pointing a pistol straight at Lord Petteril’s heart. One of the runners—Knott himself—reached for Jace, but too late, too late to stop him shooting.

Only Jace himself changed his mind at the last moment, shifting his aim to Jimmy Knott. Which was when Petteril leapt and the noise deafened her.

She cried out as Petteril and Jace crashed to the floor. She lunged toward them, knocked aside by grappling men. Frankie Sullivan, Jace's pet brute, was faster, shoving someone one out of the way and grasping Petteril by the collar. Not just to haul him off. A blade glinted in his hand. Quicker than Leeky's garrotte.

In passing, April jumped, snatched a gin bottle from the counter, and smashed it down on Frankie's head. He collapsed on top of the heap, dropping the knife, which Jimmy Knott seized before she could. Sobbing with the effort, April hauled Frankie's dead weight off Lord Petteril and threw herself down beside him. He didn't move. There was blood seeping through his coat, and his eyes were closed.

Knott sat on Jace's back, yelling for manacles.

April didn't care. Tears streaming unchecked down her cheeks she cradled Lord Petteril's head in her lap. "Don't be dead," she said wildly. "Don't you dare die!" His light could not have gone from her world; she wouldn't let it. And yet even with the thought, she knew she couldn't prevent it. All she'd won for him that first night in Petteril House was another two months.

The great, funny, eccentric life that filled her own was expiring before her eyes and she could not bear it. No grief, no loneliness had ever felt like this. She barely heard the fighting and the shouting around her.

"Don't, mister," she pleaded. "Please don't. Please..."

"It's in his pocket," Lord Petteril said in a slightly dazed voice. His eyes fluttered open, dark and unfocused. He blinked and smiled at her as though she had just popped back in from the stables in time for a reading lesson. "April."

Sheer emotion choked her. She swore at him, then swooped and pressed her lips hard to his.

Chapter Twelve

The last thing Piers had meant to do was faint. But he must have lost consciousness for at least a few moments because his eyes were closed, and he could smell April, the scent of the soap she liked so much. A drop of moisture landed on his face, and her voice whispered brokenly, "Don't, mister, please don't. Please...."

For a moment, he felt so disoriented, he couldn't tell what was happening. Then he realized the fight was still going on.

Somewhere in the wall of noise, Jimmy Knott's voice said, "That's got you, you slippery bastard."

And he knew they had Marr. Everything flooded back.

"It's in his pocket," he said urgently, but when he opened his eyes the face that swam into focus was not Knott's but April's. Which was unbearably sweet and he couldn't help smiling. Even though she was weeping and didn't seem to know whether to be furious or overjoyed. He expected it was a huge surprise to both of them when she kissed him.

He understood why she did it. She had thought he was dead. But in that moment, her kiss was everything he had ever wanted. He reached up to touch her hair by way of comfort. That she cared so much almost undid him. and gently, so gently, he returned the pressure of her mouth.

The noise in the room rolled back. Just for an instant, there was only April and Piers. But it *was* only an instant. He let his hand drop and she drew back, her deep blue eyes intense and confused.

An invisible line had been crossed.

She blinked rapidly and swallowed.

"What's in his pocket?" she asked aggressively.

That's my April. "Barret's sleeve button."

Knott uttered an exclamation and stopped hauling Marr to his feet, in order to go through his pockets. April gazed over his head, holding herself stiff as though expecting...who knew what? But her eyes lit up when Knott produced the initialled cuff link.

"Got him," she said happily. And then with sudden fury, "What you doing, getting yourself shot? I never got shot here, not *once*! Should have taken me with you, shouldn't you?"

Piers wheezed out a laugh and tried to pull himself upright. His arm hurt like the devil. Bizarrely, it was Stewart, sporting a cut above one eye, who helped him sit. April, scolding and nagging, helped Stewart wrestle him painfully out of the coat and inspected his injury.

Knott joined in. "Just grazed," he said with considerable relief. Not unnaturally, he didn't want his obsession with Marr to have caused the death of a nobleman. "Passed through the fleshy bit without touching anything too important I should think. Best see the quack, though. And keep it clean."

There was considerable satisfaction in April's face as she poured gin over the wound.

Despite the pain, a curious cloud of wellbeing had settled over Piers. It came with a sense of unreality, so he tried not to pay it too much attention. But the warmth of April fussing at his side in the hackney, was too precious to discard just yet. Stewart sat opposite them. Which was still odd.

"How do you come to be here?" Piers asked him.

"I made him tell me you'd taken the clerk's clothes," April answered for him. "He didn't know what it meant, but I did. At least you'd the sense to bring the runners."

"Were you *fighting*, Stewart?" Piers asked, gazing at the cut above his eye, and then at the grazed knuckles of his right hand.

"I had to strike one of them," Stewart said.

Piers shifted on the bench. April's closeness was very sweet. Perhaps he could allow it just this once since she had been so scared for him.

"I'm sorry," he said to Stewart. "This was hardly part of your agreed duties, but I'm grateful."

Stewart nodded, still a man of few words. But his expression was not one of anger or disgust. If anything, he looked rather pleased with himself. Perhaps he wouldn't seek another position after all.

"If you don't want to cause talk, my lord," Stewart said a moment later, handing over the cloak he had worn, "you should wear this. Can you manage to go in the front without help?"

"Of course I can."

April swung the cloak around him and fastened it at the throat. She had rather lovely little hands, especially now that the skin was softer. They were quick and capable and surprisingly gentle. Her eyes were focused on the task, but a faint flush of awareness seeped along the delicate line of her cheekbone.

"I'll go with him," she said.

"No," Stewart said. "You go in the area door."

It was not an order, more of a suggestion and yet just for an instant, April looked stricken. Because Stewart was right. For the sake of appearance and everyone's reputation, no one should even know she was with them.

"I'll walk from the corner," April muttered. "You go in the front with him. They'll have to know he's ill. Will you tell Mr. Park to send for the doctor?"

Stewart nodded. It seemed Piers had nothing to contribute, which suited him well enough now that the pain had really begun to attack. Only, he missed April's closeness as she used his stick to knock on the carriage roof. The carriage pulled up opposite the park entrance and she slid out. He had a glimpse of her white face as they pulled away. She looked so alone, so haunted that reality finally began to penetrate his foolish happiness.

What have I done?

In the morning, the slight fever that had plagued him during the night, still hung around. His wound had been cleaned and dressed by the family physician, whom he vaguely recalled, and a new dressing applied by Stewart before he helped him dress.

"Mrs. Park has laudanum for the pain," Stewart offered.

Deliberately, Piers smoothed the frown from his brow. He didn't want laudanum. It was associated in his mind with the blackness of last winter when he had been desperate to sleep and couldn't.

"It's not that bad," he said lightly. "But I was thinking I can't face the staff lessons today."

"Miss April has already cancelled today's lesson."

"Has she? How very managing," Piers said vaguely.

"And useful," Stewart pointed out.

Piers sank into the comfortable chair in his sitting room, a smile flickering on his lips in spite of himself. "And useful," he agreed.

Stewart had been at the Queen's Head. Had he seen April kiss him? Why in God's name had Piers allowed it? Now he had a mess to sort out and he doubted anyone was going to like it.

He needed to think.

But at least he was good at that.

"Where is April?"

"Helping Mrs. Park. But I believe she means to go to Kensington to call on a friend. She said you would want her to."

Piers nodded. Annie would have to know. No doubt Lord Kinsley and the rest of the Bootles would hear through official channels that Barret's murderer was in custody. He should write to Percy, too.

However, he spent the morning with his books, alternately buried deep in personal, practical thoughts and in distracting questions of history. He had not written any letters at all when Stewart brought the message that Sir Peter Haggard had called, along with Mr. and Miss Austen.

"Should Mr. Park explain you are indisposed, my lord?" Stewart asked. He waved one hand at the bulging bandage beneath Piers's shirt sleeve. "Since you are."

"No." Piers still felt a trifle woolly and a mild surge of heat accompanied the effort of his rise from the chair. "I'll go down. You'd better help me into a coat."

"I suggest this country coat."

It was looser across the shoulders and chest, and the sleeves were less fitted. "Excellent notion."

Even so, getting into it was a painful business, and he was grateful for Stewart's help. However, despite the valet's hovering, he walked downstairs unaided and into the drawing room.

"What's happened?" Haggs demanded, waving a newspaper as he leapt to his feet. "They've arrested some criminal from the rookeries for Bootle's murder!"

"Quite right, too," Piers said. He bowed to Miss Austen and dropped with some relief into the nearest chair.

Haggs peered at him. "Are you quite well, Withy?"

"Oh, just a tad under the weather," Piers said vaguely. He grinned at Austen. "But you are definitely in the clear, and so is Annie. Marr was part of her past. He wanted her back in St. Giles to help revive his flagging fortunes. He had—er... a business competitor."

"Don't see how that called for killing Bootle," Austen said, frowning.

"Well, there may have been a little more to it than that. I suspect, in his own, way, Marr cared for Annie. That was why he took the sleeve button that will hang him in the end. It had her name on it. And in an effort to shake Marr off, Annie told him that Bootle had forbidden her to pay any more money to him. So killing Barret reasserted Marr's authority, ensuring Annie would pay until she couldn't anymore and then she'd have to go back to him. Or give him the house. And he deliberately implicated her by dropping the duelling pistol beside the body. Probably so she'd turn to him for help escaping the law. Except the suspicion fell instead on Percy."

Only when he saw Miss Austen wrinkling her nose, did he realize how unsuitable these details were for a lady's ears. "Sorry," he said to her. "Distasteful in the extreme, but at least the matter is now closed."

"And we know how much of that we owe to you," she said softly. "Thank you, my lord, from the bottom of my heart. And Percy's," she added, blushing.

Piers, with his new insight, recognized that blush. For a moment, taken by surprise, he even wondered if that was his way out.

If Louise Austen, who liked him, was his way out.

After all, *he* liked *her*. And then he was ashamed. He couldn't and wouldn't do that to any of them.

"No, no," he said with deliberate vagueness. "I just follow my nose. But glad to see you cleared, Percy. Awkward time for you."

Percy rose and thrust out his hand. "Thanks, Withy. My aunt's waiting so I can't stop. But I'll get the rest out of you later!"

Piers rose again with as much grace as he could muster and bowed them out.

“Now,” Haggs said when the door closed behind him. “Sit down before you fall and tell me all.”

Piers obeyed, explaining how Gussie’s hat, once Maria’s, had given him the idea, and how he’d gone to Bow Street and formulated the plan with Jimmy Knott.

“Good God, you didn’t, did you?” Haggard said, staring, even though he’d been part of Piers’s more insane exploits when they were students. “You did! But you can’t have known Marr would have the sleeve button on him. He could have hidden it anywhere or sold it on. He could have thrown it away.”

“I know. In fact, Knott thought that with Marr under arrest, his minions would give away his hiding places, because he rarely has stolen goods on premises that can be traced to him. My hope was really to get him to say something, admit something that he couldn’t possibly know unless he had been there, or even confess to the murder.”

“Some hope. He’d only deny the confession to the law.”

Piers looked down his nose. “So? The word of a known criminal against that of Lord Petteril?”

Haggs grinned. “Fair enough.”

“I asked for an engraving to prove my artistry, but I didn’t really expect him to produce the stolen button. Anyway, my performance had drawn in most of his watchers, which was what we had hoped for, and Knott and some other runners had surrounded the building before anyone inside knew about it. Knott was sure there were other ways out, under the ground and over the roofs, but if his men got in fast enough, Marr and his cohorts wouldn’t be able to get to them. They didn’t. There was a bit of a mill, quite a rumpus, in fact, but they took Marr for murder, and hauled the rest in for affray.”

Piers’s lip quirked. “Expect the others are out again now, especially if they blabbed anything useful about Marr and his hat. I think it was Jerry Nash who wore it the night of the murder, to fool Jimmy Knott. He’s fairish like Marr, and the right height.”

“Did you get hurt in this—er...rumpus?” Haggs asked suspiciously.

“Devil a bit.” He paused, wondering how to phrase it, then just said it simply. “April was there.”

Haggs blinked. “I’m fairly sure you found her there in the first place, so I expect she was useful.”

Piers's smile felt painful, yet he couldn't stop it. "She broke a gin bottle over Frankie Sullivan's head. He's huge." The smile faded. "I upset her."

"How did you do that?" Haggs asked evenly.

"Got shot in the arm and she thought I was dead."

Haggs swore.

"I need you to do something for me," Piers said in a rush.

"Name it."

Piers adjusted his position, feeling the throb of his wound. "Do you think your stepmother would still be willing to take April? She can read and write now with increasing skill, and she's learned a good deal about housekeeping."

Haggs nodded, looking at his boots rather than at Piers. "Of course. I'm sure she would. The question is, rather, will April be prepared to go?"

Later in the afternoon, Lord Dilworth and Mrs. Bootle called.

Piers, having retreated to his own apartments again, went back downstairs to the drawing room, ordering tea on the way.

His visitors both stood as he entered the room. They were both dressed in very correct black. Mrs Bootle was veiled. She offered her hand at once and Piers bowed over it.

"Please, sit," he offered. "I believe tea is on the way. How are you both?" He glanced from one to the other.

"Grateful," Dilworth said bluntly. "I have to pass on to you my father's gratitude, too. We feel that Barret can rest in peace now that his murderer is brought to justice. For your part in that, we owe you a debt of gratitude we can never repay."

"I don't know why you should think I am involved at all," Piers said, more alarmed than modest.

"The magistrate told my father you had provided the critical evidence," Dilworth replied dryly. "I understand you did it for Austen's sake, which makes me doubly thankful."

"I can't think why," Piers said. He hoped Louise would not accept Dilworth. He might be a faithful enough husband, but in his own way he was considerably less trustworthy than Barret. Besides, Piers still could not like him. "Ah, here is tea."

It was only as they departed that Barbara Bootle made an excuse to come back into the room for her forgotten black lace shawl. Gallantly, Piers brought it to her and, awkwardly one-handed, placed it lightly across her shoulders.

"Thank you." She turned to face him, lifting her veil to look directly into his eyes. "I am leaving tomorrow for my parents' house in the country."

"Then I wish you a safe journey and peace to recover."

She searched his eyes. "I think you may have found out certain...*things* about us in your efforts to clear Mr. Austen's name."

"If I did, I have forgotten them. In any case, my discretion is absolute."

Her eyes lightened. A faint smile even twitched her lips and vanished. "I believe you. Thank you, Lord Petteril."

"There is nothing to thank me for." He bowed again and smiled. "I like Keyes. He is a good man."

She gasped, half-laughing, and whisked herself away.

The following day, Lord Petteril let it be known that he would resume reading lessons in the library. Now, April thought grimly, he will have to face me.

She knew he had been avoiding her. Admittedly, he had been weak and a bit fevered on the evening he was shot, and for most of the following day, according to Stewart. He was entitled to hide in his own apartments. But she also knew he had come down to receive Sir Peter and the Austens, and again to see Lord Dilworth and Mrs. Bootle. He hadn't sent for her at all, and that hurt, quite apart from the gnawing anxiety in her stomach.

What on earth had possessed her to kiss him? God knew what she'd brought down on herself. She had spoiled everything, changed everything. But worse by far than any of that was the fear that he would send her away.

Had she finally crossed the line of what he could or would tolerate?

Sitting at the kitchen table, toying with breakfast, she wondered if she should go early to the library, just to clear the air. Or should she linger after the lesson and try to talk to him then?

"He wants you," Francis said, arriving in the kitchen with the tray of breakfast dishes and leftovers.

Her breath caught. For an instant, she couldn't move. Then, she rose, forcing her face to give nothing away, and walked slowly out of the kitchen and upstairs.

The library door was open, so she saw at once that he stood by the window. His back was straight, the slight bulge around his left arm the only sign of his injury beneath the looser than usual coat that he had worn frequently at Haybury Court. His hair looked untidier than usual, as if he had been dragging his fingers through it, or at least refused to let Stewart brush it. She wondered what he did let Stewart do.

Change the dressings on his arm.

"Close the door," he said without turning.

His voice was not encouraging. She obeyed, her heart sinking, then wiped her hands almost convulsively on her skirts.

He turned, flapping one hand at the chairs they usually sat in to discuss things. She sat, and after a moment, so did he.

"I've been thinking," he said abruptly, "about your future. I have decided it would be best if you went now to Lady Haggard, who can train you far better than I can."

She stared at him, though he couldn't know since his gaze was on the empty grate, not on her. "Best for whom?" she asked mulishly. "Train me for what?"

For an instant, as his eyes lightened and a smile flickered across his face, she thought it would be fine after all.

"I hope she will be as impressed as I am at the improvement in your grammar."

"She don't care about my bleeding grammar." *Or me.*

"She will care about the swearing."

"She won't have to. I ain't going."

He sighed, and the sheer patience in it appalled her. This was how he spoke to his disrespectful cousins and his aunt when he could no longer be bothered with their rudeness. It felt like a slap in the face. Was she truly no more than that?

With cool deliberation, he raised his eyes from the fireplace to her face. They were cold and hard. She had seen that before, too, though never directed at her. Something shrivelled inside her.

"You will go," he said with calm certainty.

"Why?" Sheer desperation lent her courage. She had nothing to lose now. "Because I kissed you?"

He hadn't expected her to bring it up. Or perhaps he had just hoped. At any rate, a faint flush stained his pale cheeks, and he wrenched his gaze free.

"Yes," he said coldly.

But his eyes were not cold. His mouth was too...stiff. He was hiding. He was...vulnerable.

And everything—*everything*—depended on how she reacted now.

"Sometimes you're an ass, mister," she said with friendly scorn. "I was just glad you were alive after all. Thought you'd croaked. Don't mean no more n' that, so don't go thinking I'm *encroaching*, about to inveigling you into bed. We ain't like that, you and me."

She wanted to get up and do something, so that he wouldn't see her face, but she was too afraid of not seeing his.

There had been an instant, in the Queen's Head, when she had felt his lips move under hers, kissing her back. It was that memory that made her heart beat so violently—the hope, the happiness that would die if he sent her away now.

His eyes bored into hers with all their old sharpness, and then, abruptly, they closed.

He got up. "No, we ain't like that," he agreed in a rush. "The trouble here is propriety, April."

"I don't care about that."

"I know you don't. So I have to care for you. We walk a tightrope here, and that is my fault. I have made your place in my household ambivalent, and before you tell me that doesn't matter, consider that Stewart was in the Queen's Head."

It was her turn to blush, but she tilted her chin to show how little she minded that either.

He tried again. "You and I are constantly getting into situations where one of us has to rescue the other. What happened at the Queen's Head, or something very like it, was inevitable and will not do, because whatever it is, our relationship is inappropriate."

"Because you're the viscount and I'm only a thief from the St. Giles gutters?"

His lips quirked at last with a blessed hint of humour. "There's no *only* about you, April. And no. Because I am the master and you the servant I pay."

"Most gents don't mind that. The servants are fair game. I like your honour, but—"

"It's not just my honour, it's yours," he said impatiently. "You need a life without me and you won't have it if I've soiled your reputation. However innocently."

She glared at him. "Ever think of consulting *me*? You keep telling me that I can choose, that everything's my choice, only it never is, is it? You made me be a girl when I didn't want to be and now—"

"Well, that's worked out fine, hasn't it?" he interrupted.

"Yes," she admitted with difficulty. She took a deep breath. "I didn't feel safe as a girl. Before. I do now."

He took a step nearer her and stopped, a dire frown tugging down his brow. "That's the other reason, April. I *want* you to be safe. To feel safe."

He knew. Or he guessed.

She licked her dry lips, avoiding his gaze now. "Did Annie tell you about me?"

"Does Annie know about you?" he countered.

"She guesses." And so did he. It was in his dark, pitying eyes, damn him. She should have known. She wanted to crawl away and hide beneath the ground.

He must have seen the instinctive, protective curl of her body because suddenly he dropped down in front of her chair.

"No," he said fiercely. "Never, never imagine your past makes you unclean. *The shame is not yours,* April."

She stared at him, uncomprehending. Her throat closed up. "But you're sending me away," she gasped.

Now he looked truly appalled. And she realized with astonishment that at last, when she wasn't trying, she held the key in her hand.

"Not for that," he whispered. "Dear God, April, did I not say it's for your safety? You have to be safe—" He broke off abruptly, and the incredible thought struck her that he wanted her to be safe *from him*.

She hadn't imagined that moment in the Queen's Head, but if she wanted to stay with him, she had to forget it.

"You have to be safe," he finished more calmly.

"I'm safe here. I always felt safe with you. I trust you. And I like being your assistant. I'm useful. All we need to do is be a bit more careful, so no idiots think we're *inappropriate*." She took a breath. "You can begin by getting off your knees, because Gawd knows what Francis and Jenny would make of *that*."

A breath of laughter shook him, though he stumbled upright without his usual grace.

She brushed past him. "Will I set out the books?"

There was only a very faint pause before he said, "Yes. Set out the books."

Her shoulders relaxed. For an instant, her back to him, she closed her eyes in relief so powerful that it hurt.

But it was going to be fine. She would stay.

Lord Petteril Mysteries

Have you read the other Lord Petteril Mysteries?

- Petteril's Thief
- Petteril's Corpse
- Petteril's Ladybird

(Read on for an excerpt from Book 1, Petteril's Thief...)

Excerpt from Petteril's Thief

The small thief known as Ape froze in a sudden draught.

As though a window had suddenly blown open.

Abandoning the lantern and the calico bag into which he had been happily stuffing a roll of paper money and a few elegant sleeve buttons from the open safe chest, the boy crept out of the dressing room and into the main bedchamber. And his stomach seemed to lunge up into his throat.

One of the full-length French windows had indeed blown open, lifting the curtain and admitting a suddenly bright patch of moonlight. Through the glass, the thief could see the outline of a small, stone balcony and a man's tall, slender back.

Gawd All Mighty! How did I miss that cove?

The only thing to do was grab the bag, get out as fast as he could, and face Lord's temper at such meagre pickings. Except for some reason, there seemed more wrong here than an empty house that wasn't empty at all. The man on the balcony looked well dressed like any nob, and his profile was that of a young man. Yet his shoulders were stooped like someone old and weary, and he seemed to be swaying.

Gawd's bottom, is he bosky? Drunk enough to fall over the balustrade?

Heart in his mouth, Ape took a step closer, and then another. *I must be dicked in the nob...* He found himself almost at the window, but the man didn't seem to see or hear him. Worse, Ape recalled that they were three floors up, and here at the back of the house, the flag-stoned yard directly below dipped even beneath the basement kitchen. If this drunken fool fell over, he would die.

And he was going to. He swayed toward the balustrade with such sudden force that Ape knew he would go straight over. Before he could stop himself, Ape dived out the window, grabbed the fellow's hand and hauled him back.

The drunk didn't even seem surprised. In fact, he seemed reluctant to turn his head, though he finally did, blinking at Ape as though not quite seeing him.

Well, if he's that jug-bitten, perhaps he won't remember me, Ape thought optimistically. For good measure, he hauled the man through the window, which he shut and locked.

The drunk, eerily illuminated in the shaft of moonlight through the glass, was still gazing at him, a faint frown forming between eyes that seemed to be gaining in focus. "Who the devil are you?"

"Who the devil are *you*?" Ape retorted, "Some drunk wandered in off the street? You want to go home, you do. You'll have a head thick as a turnip in the morning." Even as he said the words, it came to him that the man did not smell of drink. Nor, apart from the swaying, did he move like a drunk.

The man ambled past him, and Ape heard the sound of flint striking before the glow of several candles sprung up. Ape hadn't even seen the candle sticks. They were probably silver. Lord would want those.

"What you doing up here in the dark anyway?" Ape asked in severe tones as he backed toward the door. "Never tell me you own this ken?"

The man, who was tall and thin, his clothes decent if hardly the first stare of fashion, blinked at him. His face was handsome enough with its high forehead, long nose and well-defined bones, yet it looked sad and bleak to Ape. His shock of curly hair, the colour of chestnuts in autumn, was dishevelled and untidy. Even the dark, dark eyes held a hint of desperation, although Ape didn't know how they could give the impression of being both perceptive and utterly vague at the same time. The man turned his head, as though distracted, looking toward the dressing room where the lantern still shone on Ape's bag of meagre loot.

Hell and the devil! He'd nearly forgotten it. Hastily, Ape changed direction and swaggered toward the bag. "Well?" he said aggressively, referring to his last question in the hope of distracting his unwanted companion.

The man appeared to think about it. "It wasn't dark when I arrived," he said vaguely, while Ape swiped up the bag. "And yes, apparently so."

Ape knew better than to believe a word of it. "Well, stay away from windows till you're sober," he advised.

The faintest of smiles flickered across the man's face without lightening it in the least. "I don't suppose you found any brandy?" he said, nodding at Ape's bag.

Ape stopped swaggering, noting that the man now stood between him and the door. "No," he said brazenly. "Empty, dreary kind of place. Inhospitable."

"True," the man agreed. He held out his hand.

Ape looked at it, then at the man, sizing up his speed and strength. Not quick, he decided, not in this state, but definitely bigger than Ape. And in the way. "Split it with you?" he said hopefully.

The man said nothing. His hand remained steady.

With a sigh, Ape handed over the bag. "Lord's going to kill me now."

"The good Lord?" the man said, rummaging in the bag among the bits of lace, silk and linen without obvious interest.

"Nah," Ape said and decided, reluctantly, to scare off the gentleman. "He's a bowman prig, Lord is."

"Prig," the man repeated, more thoughtfully. "Thief? Burglar?"

"That's it. Powerful mean he is, too."

"You can't like working for someone powerful mean," the man observed.

"I don't," Ape admitted. "But a man has to eat."

His unwanted companion looked up from his haphazard poking about in the bag and examined Ape with the first glimmerings of real intelligence. "A man," he repeated. "How old are you?"

Ape shrugged. "Don't know."

"How'd you get in? Pick the lock on the back door?"

"Nah, we're not on the dub lay. Trigged the jigger yesterday, like, to see the place was empty, then milled the glaze on the pantry so I could wriggle in through the bars."

The gentleman regarded him with some fascination. His lips even twitched and there might have been some light in those bleak eyes. Ape felt ridiculously pleased.

"You didn't pick the lock," the man guessed. "I'm going to ignore the jigger and guess you broke the pantry window. You were sent inside to do the work while your Lord snoozes outside."

"He don't snooze," Ape said. "He looks out for the Watch, or anyone coming home."

"Slim pickings." The man let the bag dangle from his slender hand. "What's your name?"

"Ape. Won't do you no good. They'll never find me."

"Who won't?"

"The Watch! The Runners! Mister, are you dicked in the nob?"

Again, his lips twitched. "That one I know, and yes, probably." Unexpectedly, he tossed the bag to Ape, who only just caught it, and stepped aside. "Shab off, then."

Ape could not believe his luck and stared at the gentleman. He hadn't even taken the money from the bag, or the gold cuff links.

"Shab *straight* off," the man clarified.

"What are you going to do?" Ape blurted.

"Sleep," the gentleman said, and actually lay down on top of the bed.

Ape blinked at him owlishly for a moment, then went and blew out the candles before collecting his lantern and hurrying away. In the passage, he felt moved to close the door, and glanced first at the still, dark mound on the bed. He might already have been asleep.

Totally dicked in the nob. But he'd saved Ape a thrashing and so Ape would tell no one about his presence.

(Read the rest in *Petteril's Thief*, available now)

Crime & Passion

Another historical mystery series by Mary Lancaster.

London, 1851... In the shadow of the Great Exhibition, poverty and crime stalk the meaner backstreets of the city. But sin is not confined to the underworld. One couple passes seamlessly between the neighbouring worlds of privilege and privation, solving crimes and enabling love to bloom.

Mysterious Lover
Letters to a Lover
Dangerous Lover
Lost Lover
https://marylancaster.com/books/#historicalmysteries

About the Author

Mary Lancaster is a USA Today bestselling author of award winning historical romance and historical fiction. She lives in Scotland with her husband, one of three grown-up kids, and a small dog with a big personality.

Her first literary love was historical fiction, a genre which she relishes mixing up with romance and adventure in her own writing. Several of her novels feature actual historical characters as diverse as Hungarian revolutionaries, medieval English outlaws, and a family of eternally rebellious royal Scots. To say nothing of Vlad the Impaler.

More recently, she has enjoyed writing light, fun Regency romances, with occasional forays into the Victorian era. With its slight change of emphasis, *Petteril's Thief*, is her first Regency-set historical mystery.

Connect with Mary on-line – she loves to hear from readers:

Email Mary: Mary@MaryLancaster.com

Website: http://www.MaryLancaster.com

Newsletter sign-up: https://marylancaster.com/newsletter/

Facebook: https://www.facebook.com/mary.lancaster.1656

Facebook Author Page:
https://www.facebook.com/MaryLancasterNovelist/

Twitter: @MaryLancNovels
https://twitter.com/MaryLancNovels

Bookbub: https://www.bookbub.com/profile/mary-lancaster

Printed in Great Britain
by Amazon

40409545R00078